再 版 序

教育部推展的「**全民英語能力認證**」制度，肯定民眾在學校以外的各種學習成就，教育部並委託語言中心規畫一套具公信力的認證、檢定制度，高中學生畢業時均須參加「中級英語能力檢定測驗」，高中在校生最好提早準備此項考試。

英語能力分級檢定測驗依不同英語程度，分爲初、中、中高、高和優等五級，預計測驗時間爲兩個小時，一般民眾通過中級英語能力檢定測驗之後，可以此做爲就業或申請學校的證明。教育部待這項測驗發展穩定後，結合大學入學考試，擴充認證制度功能。

這一冊書共分爲八回，每回考試時間爲 40 分鐘，每回測驗分爲四部份，和教育部的中級英語檢定測驗相同。這八回測驗，每回都經過劉毅英文聽力班實際考試，以每題 1.67 分計算，最高分介於 79 分至 86 分之間，最低分介於 35 至 42 分之間。每份考題能考 60 分以上，算及格。本試題比實際考試多一項，本書的第四部份是針對「大學入學推薦甄試」所設計，讀者也可以藉此考驗自己的能力，出乎其上，必得其中。

本書是依據「**英語能力分級檢定**」測驗指標，在單字爲五千字的範圍內，可聽懂對話及廣播。要在聽力一項得高分，就是要不斷練習，現在在校的高中學生，早晚都要參加此項考試，要及早準備，爲學校爭光。本書另附有教師手冊。本書第二冊也已出版，老師可將本書第一冊發給學生練習，第二冊作爲考試用。

編輯好書是「學習」一貫的宗旨。本書在編審及校對的每一階段，均力求完善，但恐有疏漏之處，誠盼各界先進，不吝批評指正。

劉 毅

本書製作過程

Test Book No. 1, 4, 7 由蔡琇瑩老師負責，Test Book No. 2, 5, 8 由高瑋謙老師負責， No. 3, 6 由謝靜芳老師負責。每份試題均由三位老師，在聽力班實際測驗過，經過每週一次測驗後，立刻講解的方式，學生們的聽力有明顯的進步，在大學甄試聽力考試中，都輕鬆過關。三位老師們的共同看法是，要在聽力方面得高分，就要不斷練習，愈多愈好。聽力訓練，愈早開始愈好。

本書另附有教師手冊，附有答案及詳解，售價 180 元。
錄音帶八卷，售價 960 元。

English Listening Comprehension Test

Test Book No. 1

This listening comprehension test will test your ability to understand spoken English. In this test, each conversation, statement and question will be spoken JUST ONE TIME. They will not be written out for you. There are four parts to this test. Special instructions will be given to you at the beginning of each part.

Part A

In Part A, you will see several pictures in your test book. For each picture, you will be asked 1 to 3 questions. For each question, you will hear four possible answers. Choose the best answer according to what you see in the picture.

Example:

You will see:

You will hear: What is this?

A. This is a table.
B. This is a chair.
C. This is a watch.
D. This is a doll.

The best answer to the question "What is this?" is B: "This is a chair." Therefore, you should choose answer B.

A. Questions 1-2

E. Questions 9-10

B. Questions 3-4

F. Questions 11-12

C. Questions 5-6

G. Question 13

D. Questions 7-8

H. Questions 14-15

Part B

In Part B, you will hear 15 questions. After you hear a question, read the four possible answers in your test book and decide which one is the best answer to the question you have heard.

Example:

You will hear: What does your father do?

You will read:
A. He's 50 years old.
B. He's a teacher.
C. He's hungry.
D. He's in Los Angeles.

The best answer to the question "What does your father do?" is B: "He's a teacher." Therefore, you should choose answer B.

Please go to the next page.

16. A. Yes, it's yours.
    B. No, it's not his.
    C. No, it's mine.
    D. No, it's yours.

17. A. You are welcome.
    B. No, thanks.
    C. No, I didn't help you.
    D. How about you?

18. A. Is it real?
    B. I am sorry to hear that.
    C. I don't hear that.
    D. I don't know your father.

19. A. It is a good class.
    B. I like that class.
    C. There are fifty students in that class.
    D. It starts at eight-thirty.

20. A. No, I have one brother.
    B. Yes, I have one sister.
    C. No, I have.
    D. Yes, I have one.

21. A. It's Peter's.
    B. He is an American boy.
    C. It's me, Bill.
    D. Oh, are you my neighbor?

22. A. Sure. You're right.
    B. How did you do it?
    C. Can you do that?
    D. Cheer up! Work harder next time.

23. A. No, they are not interested.
    B. No, it is boring.
    C. Yes, it is interested.
    D. Yes, it is boring.

24. A. Yes, I can give you both hands.
    B. I'm sorry. I'm busy now.
    C. That's a good idea.
    D. No, I can't lend my hand.

25. A. Are you Helen?
    B. Is that Helen?
    C. That's not Helen.
    D. This is Helen.

26. A. It's very hot today.
    B. It's a fine day.
    C. It's March 10.
    D. It's Friday.

27. A. Here are they.
    B. Here they are.
    C. Here it is.
    D. Here are you.

28. A. He likes art.
    B. He's from Keelung.
    C. He gets up at six.
    D. He is a teacher.

29. A. The weekend was too short.
    B. That's all right.
    C. We had a good time.
    D. I liked it.

30. A. It won't bite.
    B. It is bigger.
    C. It is broken.
    D. It is expensive.

Part C

In Part C, you will hear 15 conversations between a man and a woman. After each conversation, you will hear a question about the conversation. After you hear the question, read the four possible answers in your test book and choose the best answer to the question you have heard.

Example:

You will hear: (Man) How do you go to school every day?
(Woman) Usually by bus. Sometimes by taxi.

TONE: How does the woman go to school?

You will read:
A. She always goes to school on foot.
B. She usually takes a bike.
C. She takes either a bus or a taxi.
D. She usually goes to school by bus, never by taxi.

The best answer to the question "How does the woman go to school?" is C: "She takes either a bus or a taxi." Therefore, you should choose answer C.

Please go to the next page. ⇨

31. A. It will depend on the weather.
    B. He has a better idea.
    C. He wants to be invited.
    D. That's a lot to fit into one day.

32. A. A new medicine for headaches.
    B. A class they're taking.
    C. The man's job.
    D. The man's health.

33. A. Laura really needs a full-time job.
    B. Laura already has a job working for the school.
    C. Laura needs to spend her time studying.
    D. Laura should think about becoming a teacher.

34. A. Look for another seat.
    B. Repeat the question.
    C. Remain standing.
    D. Sit down.

35. A. Put sugar in the tea.
    B. Excuse him.
    C. Repeat what she said.
    D. Allow him to pass.

36. A. Professor Janson has won a million dollars.
    B. Professor Janson is lucky to be teaching at that school.
    C. Teachers like Professor Janson are rare.
    D. There are a great many teachers of Professor Janson's subject.

37. A. She's always running.
    B. She's still in the race.
    C. She feels very comfortable.
    D. She still has a fever.

38. A. How much time the job will take.
    B. How the man's health is.
    C. What the man is going to do.
    D. If the weather is good today.

39. A. He likes to keep his car looking beautiful.
    B. He wonders who their next neighbor will be.
    C. He admires the neighbor's car.
    D. He hasn't met the new neighbor yet.

40. A. He needs to sleep for three or four hours.
    B. He wants to buy a set of coffee cups.
    C. He will need more than one cup of coffee.
    D. He has been wide awake for some time.

41. A. She wants to borrow his dictionary.
    B. She doesn't know which word he means.
    C. He shouldn't use such big words.
    D. He should look the word up in a dictionary.

42. A. He gets nervous when he goes to dinner parties.
    B. He eats when he needs to calm down.
    C. He thinks the other sandwich would be much better.
    D. He wants the woman to eat the rest of the food.

43. A. Marge has gone home.
    B. Marge feels at home there.
    C. He's known Marge for a long time.
    D. He just met Marge.

44. A. Shelley knows someone there.
    B. Shelley didn't tell him.
    C. He doesn't know who Shelley is.
    D. He wonders which way Shelley went.

45. A. There will be a lot of rain.
    B. Rain is very unlikely.
    C. It's already raining.
    D. She's not sure.

Part D

In Part D, you will hear 15 short talks. After each talk, you will hear a question about the talk. After you hear the question, read the four possible answers in your test book and choose the best answer to the question you have heard.

Example:

You will hear: Well, that's all for Unit 15. For today's homework, please do the review questions on page 80, and we'll check the answers tomorrow. Now, let's go on to Unit 16.

TONE: What is the teacher going to do next in today's class?

You will read: A. Check the homework.
B. Review Unit 15.
C. Start a new unit.
D. Answer students' questions.

The best answer to the question "What is the teacher going to do next in today's class?" is C: "Start a new unit." Therefore, you should choose answer C.

Please go to the next page. ⇨

46. A. He ate spoiled food.
B. He ate uncooked food.
C. He didn't cook food long enough.
D. He ate food just gotten out of the oven.

47. A. Children's play balloons.
B. Weather balloons.
C. Balloons used for safety patrols.
D. Balloons used for recreation.

48. A. Because she'd been born that way.
B. Because a horse had kicked her.
C. Because she'd had a very high fever.
D. Because she'd had a bad fall.

49. A. Fifty yards.
B. Fifty laps.
C. Once around the yard.
D. One length of the pool.

50. A. Because he felt strongly about slavery.
B. Because he was defeated by Lincoln for president.
C. Because he was short in stature but strong in frame.
D. Because his head was larger than his shoulders.

51. A. On the first day of class.
B. At the end of the first week of classes.
C. Halfway through the semester.
D. Just before the final exam.

52. A. Russian.
B. German.
C. French.
D. Polish.

53. A. Cool.
B. Warm.
C. Cloudy.
D. Sunny.

54. A. The editor.
B. A journalism professor.
C. The budget director.
D. An engineer.

55. A. Commercial fishing.
B. Biology.
C. Mechanical engineering.
D. Computer programming.

56. A. Bicycles and cars.
B. Building codes.
C. Energy conservation.
D. New housing construction.

57. A. The life of Emily Dickinson.
B. The poetry of Walt Whitman.
C. The work of Professor May.
D. The life of Walt Whitman.

58. A. Students.
B. Government officials.
C. City planners.
D. Fishermen.

59. A. After class.
B. At the beginning of the term.
C. In the fall.
D. Before vacation.

60. A. 1588.
B. 1603.
C. 1683.
D. 1688.

中級英語聽力檢定測驗答案紙

中文姓名 ____________________　　　　測驗日期：民國 _____ 年 _____ 月 _____ 日

1. 准考證號碼					2. 出生						3. 國民身分證統一編號									
					年(民國)		月		日											
請依序將每個數字在下欄塗黑																				
⓪①②③④⑤⑥⑦⑧⑨	⓪①②③④⑤⑥⑦⑧⑨	⓪①②③④⑤⑥⑦⑧⑨	⓪①②③④⑤⑥⑦⑧⑨	⓪①②③④⑤⑥⑦⑧⑨	⓪①②③④⑤⑥⑦⑧⑨	⓪①②③④⑤⑥⑦⑧⑨	⓪①	⓪①②③④⑤⑥⑦⑧⑨	⓪①②③	⓪①②③④⑤⑥⑦⑧⑨	ⒶⒷⒸⒹⒺⒻⒼⒽⒾⒿⓀⓁⓂⓃⓄⓅⓆⓇⓈⓉⓊⓋⓌⓍⓎⓏ	⓪①②③④⑤⑥⑦⑧⑨	⓪①②③④⑤⑥⑦⑧⑨	⓪①②③④⑤⑥⑦⑧⑨	⓪①②③④⑤⑥⑦⑧⑨	⓪①②③④⑤⑥⑦⑧⑨	⓪①②③④⑤⑥⑦⑧⑨	⓪①②③④⑤⑥⑦⑧⑨	⓪①②③④⑤⑥⑦⑧⑨	⓪①②③④⑤⑥⑦⑧⑨

＊注意：本答案紙限用 #2 (HB) 黑色鉛筆在「○」內塗黑、塗滿。

作答樣例：正確　ⒶⒷ●Ⓓ

錯誤　ⒶⒷ✓Ⓓ　ⒶⒷ✗Ⓓ　ⒶⒷ○Ⓓ　ⒶⒷ●Ⓓ

聽力測驗				
試題別				
試題冊號碼				

1 ⒶⒷⒸⒹ	11 ⒶⒷⒸⒹ	21 ⒶⒷⒸⒹ	31 ⒶⒷⒸⒹ	41 ⒶⒷⒸⒹ	51 ⒶⒷⒸⒹ
2 ⒶⒷⒸⒹ	12 ⒶⒷⒸⒹ	22 ⒶⒷⒸⒹ	32 ⒶⒷⒸⒹ	42 ⒶⒷⒸⒹ	52 ⒶⒷⒸⒹ
3 ⒶⒷⒸⒹ	13 ⒶⒷⒸⒹ	23 ⒶⒷⒸⒹ	33 ⒶⒷⒸⒹ	43 ⒶⒷⒸⒹ	53 ⒶⒷⒸⒹ
4 ⒶⒷⒸⒹ	14 ⒶⒷⒸⒹ	24 ⒶⒷⒸⒹ	34 ⒶⒷⒸⒹ	44 ⒶⒷⒸⒹ	54 ⒶⒷⒸⒹ
5 ⒶⒷⒸⒹ	15 ⒶⒷⒸⒹ	25 ⒶⒷⒸⒹ	35 ⒶⒷⒸⒹ	45 ⒶⒷⒸⒹ	55 ⒶⒷⒸⒹ
6 ⒶⒷⒸⒹ	16 ⒶⒷⒸⒹ	26 ⒶⒷⒸⒹ	36 ⒶⒷⒸⒹ	46 ⒶⒷⒸⒹ	56 ⒶⒷⒸⒹ
7 ⒶⒷⒸⒹ	17 ⒶⒷⒸⒹ	27 ⒶⒷⒸⒹ	37 ⒶⒷⒸⒹ	47 ⒶⒷⒸⒹ	57 ⒶⒷⒸⒹ
8 ⒶⒷⒸⒹ	18 ⒶⒷⒸⒹ	28 ⒶⒷⒸⒹ	38 ⒶⒷⒸⒹ	48 ⒶⒷⒸⒹ	58 ⒶⒷⒸⒹ
9 ⒶⒷⒸⒹ	19 ⒶⒷⒸⒹ	29 ⒶⒷⒸⒹ	39 ⒶⒷⒸⒹ	49 ⒶⒷⒸⒹ	59 ⒶⒷⒸⒹ
10 ⒶⒷⒸⒹ	20 ⒶⒷⒸⒹ	30 ⒶⒷⒸⒹ	40 ⒶⒷⒸⒹ	50 ⒶⒷⒸⒹ	60 ⒶⒷⒸⒹ

English Listening Comprehension Test

Test Book No. 2

This listening comprehension test will test your ability to understand spoken English. In this test, each conversation, statement and question will be spoken JUST ONE TIME. They will not be written out for you. There are four parts to this test. Special instructions will be given to you at the beginning of each part.

Part A

In Part A, you will see several pictures in your test book. For each picture, you will be asked 1 to 3 questions. For each question, you will hear four possible answers. Choose the best answer according to what you see in the picture.

Example:

You will see:

You will hear: What is this?

A. This is a table.
B. This is a chair.
C. This is a watch.
D. This is a doll.

The best answer to the question "What is this?" is B: "This is a chair." Therefore, you should choose answer B.

A. Questions 1-3

B. Questions 4-6

C. Questions 7-9

D. Questions 10-12

E. Questions 13-15

Part B

In Part B, you will hear 15 questions. After you hear a question, read the four possible answers in your test book and decide which one is the best answer to the question you have heard.

Example:

You will hear: What does your father do?

You will read: A. He's 50 years old.
B. He's a teacher.
C. He's hungry.
D. He's in Los Angeles.

The best answer to the question "What does your father do?" is B: "He's a teacher." Therefore, you should choose answer B.

Please go to the next page. ⇨

16. A. Yes, just name it.
    B. Well, it depends.
    C. Certainly. What can I do for you?
    D. Yes, of course. I wouldn't.

17. A. Many thanks.
    B. I have enough time to go shopping.
    C. So am I.
    D. My watch says eleven-forty.

18. A. Yes, I was.
    B. No, I did.
    C. Yes, I didn't.
    D. Certainly not.

19. A. Of course, I will.
    B. Thanks. Have one, too.
    C. That's it.
    D. Not at all.

20. A. I'll eat what is here.
    B. Pass me an apple, please.
    C. Thank you. I've had enough.
    D. It seems a bit thin.

21. A. Don't thank.
    B. Certainly.
    C. You're welcome.
    D. No thanks.

22. A. In English.
    B. Every four days.
    C. Three days on foot.
    D. A week once.

23. A. I play chess.
    B. I didn't like to watch TV.
    C. Why? Will you play tennis with me?
    D. Maybe you know it better than I do.

24. A. He comes from his home.
    B. He is American.
    C. He comes from the store.
    D. From Taipei. He is a Japanese.

25. A. Where, where.
    B. Thank you.
    C. You're welcome.
    D. Of course.

26. A. Yesterday morning.
    B. Something about my English homework.
    C. Because he knew my father.
    D. You are telling me.

27. A. I'm glad you enjoyed it.
    B. Welcome!
    C. Hope that you can give me one.
    D. No, thanks.

28. A. No, he is.
    B. No, he doesn't.
    C. Yes, he is.
    D. Yes, he does.

29. A. How dreadful!
    B. Better luck next time.
    C. It can't be helped.
    D. How funny.

30. A. Yes, I always have tea for breakfast.
    B. Well, can I get you anything else?
    C. I think many people drink too much.
    D. I'll have the same again, please.

Part C

In Part C, you will hear 15 conversations between a man and a woman. After each conversation, you will hear a question about the conversation. After you hear the question, read the four possible answers in your test book and choose the best answer to the question you have heard.

Example:

You will hear: (Man) How do you go to school every day?
(Woman) Usually by bus. Sometimes by taxi.

TONE: How does the woman go to school?

You will read:
A. She always goes to school on foot.
B. She usually takes a bike.
C. She takes either a bus or a taxi.
D. She usually goes to school by bus, never by taxi.

The best answer to the question "How does the woman go to school?" is C: "She takes either a bus or a taxi." Therefore, you should choose answer C.

Please go to the next page. ⇨

31. A. He has found someone else to go to the concert with him.
    B. The woman should have contacted him earlier.
    C. He is looking for someone to go to the concert with him.
    D. The woman has to find someone else to go to the concert with.

32. A. He wants to buy film.
    B. He wants to have the pictures enlarged.
    C. He wants to get some film developed.
    D. He wants a negative to be printed.

33. A. He wants to get medicine.
    B. He wants to fill out the prescription.
    C. He wants to get information on a prescription.
    D. He wants to see a doctor.

34. A. She hasn't talked with the manager yet.
    B. The new manager was not in the office.
    C. The woman has been at home.
    D. The woman didn't want to talk with the new manager.

35. A. She wants him to go to the office now.
    B. She wants him to wait.
    C. She wants him to hang up the phone.
    D. She wants him to come back at three.

36. A. Hang up the phone.
    B. Call her friend immediately.
    C. Get the telephone right now.
    D. Pass the CPA exam as Bob did.

37. A. On the table in the living room.
    B. In the man's office.
    C. In the living room.
    D. At Bob's home.

38. A. Put the sofa on the stereo.
    B. Move the sofa.
    C. Take the sofa out of the room.
    D. Buy a smaller sofa.

39. A. Asking some other people to help with the move instead of him.
    B. Finding a different apartment.
    C. Trying to find others to help her too.
    D. Asking club members to find some other apartment.

40. A. She is confident of passing the test.
    B. She is not really ready but she thinks she will pass the test.
    C. She is not really a good student but she will pass the test.
    D. She is ready for the test and will get good grades.

41. A. Stop at the grocery store.
    B. Use them in his office.
    C. Take them with him for lunch.
    D. Borrow them from his neighbor.

42. A. He is coming down with a cold, so he doesn't want to go.
    B. He is no longer ill but he wants to take care of himself.
    C. He wants to give a new flute to Susan, so he will go to the party.
    D. He doesn't want to go because he wants to practice the flute.

43. A. To make a room reservation.
    B. To pack many items in a box.
    C. To cancel the plane tickets for two.
    D. To put one small item in her suitcase.

44. A. The woman may have made a mistake.
    B. The woman actually saw the singer.
    C. The woman thought the singer is in town.
    D. The woman should go to San Francisco

45. A. Mary may not come to the party.
    B. Probably Mary will invite the woman first.
    C. Mary will probably come to the woman's party.
    D. The man will ask Mary to go to the party

Part D

In Part D, you will hear 15 short talks. After each talk, you will hear a question about the talk. After you hear the question, read the four possible answers in your test book and choose the best answer to the question you have heard.

Example:

<u>You will hear</u>: Well, that's all for Unit 15. For today's homework, please do the review questions on page 80, and we'll check the answers tomorrow. Now, let's go on to Unit 16.

TONE: What is the teacher going to do next in today's class?

<u>You will read</u>: A. Check the homework.
B. Review Unit 15.
C. Start a new unit.
D. Answer students' questions.

The best answer to the question "What is the teacher going to do next in today's class?" is C: "Start a new unit." Therefore, you should choose answer C.

Please go to the next page. ⇨

46. A. 1920.
    B. 1928.
    C. 1950.
    D. 1955.

47. A. It is close to the coastline.
    B. It has good soil.
    C. It has a large labor supply.
    D. It has the proper climate.

48. A. A magazine.
    B. A neighborhood.
    C. A period of time.
    D. A political issue.

49. A. Christmas.
    B. New Year's Day.
    C. Easter.
    D. The summer solstice.

50. A. By supporting conservation laws.
    B. By using them frequently.
    C. By using their natural resources.
    D. By increasing their animal populations.

51. A. Mr. Rockford.
    B. Mr. Rockford's friend.
    C. The receptionist.
    D. Mr. Rockford's boss.

52. A. It is self-service.
    B. It is cheap.
    C. It is high quality.
    D. It is available in schools.

53. A. At a residence.
    B. From his local fire department.
    C. From Underwriters' Laboratories.
    D. At a hardware store.

54. A. Workers may not smoke while they work.
    B. Workers may not smoke in the factory.
    C. Workers may only smoke in certain places in the factory.
    D. Workers may only smoke in certain places outside the factory.

55. A. A locksmith.
    B. A car rental agency.
    C. A gas station.
    D. A bookstore.

56. A. The regular staff.
    B. Hotel guests.
    C. Temporary workers.
    D. Female customers.

57. A. On Flight 437.
    B. In Montreal.
    C. At an airport.
    D. In a park.

58. A. On a train.
    B. In a park.
    C. On a platform.
    D. In a store.

59. A. A member of the Blasters.
    B. A radio DJ.
    C. A Romance Records spokesman.
    D. A movie star.

60. A. An insurance company.
    B. A travel agency.
    C. A golf course.
    D. A news agency.

中級英語聽力檢定測驗答案紙

中文姓名 ____________________　　　　測驗日期：民國 _____ 年 _____ 月 _____ 日

1. 准考證號碼					2. 出生 年(民國)		月		日		3. 國民身分證統一編號									
請依序將每個數字在下欄塗黑																				
⓪	⓪	⓪	⓪	⓪	⓪	⓪	⓪	⓪	⓪	⓪	Ⓐ	⓪	⓪	⓪	⓪	⓪	⓪	⓪	⓪	⓪
①	①	①	①	①	①	①	①	①	①	①	Ⓑ	①	①	①	①	①	①	①	①	①
②	②	②	②	②	②	②		②	②	②	Ⓒ	②	②	②	②	②	②	②	②	②
③	③	③	③	③	③	③		③	③	③	Ⓓ	③	③	③	③	③	③	③	③	③
④	④	④	④	④	④	④		④		④	Ⓔ	④	④	④	④	④	④	④	④	④
⑤	⑤	⑤	⑤	⑤	⑤	⑤		⑤		⑤	Ⓕ	⑤	⑤	⑤	⑤	⑤	⑤	⑤	⑤	⑤
⑥	⑥	⑥	⑥	⑥	⑥	⑥		⑥		⑥	Ⓖ	⑥	⑥	⑥	⑥	⑥	⑥	⑥	⑥	⑥
⑦	⑦	⑦	⑦	⑦	⑦	⑦		⑦		⑦	Ⓗ	⑦	⑦	⑦	⑦	⑦	⑦	⑦	⑦	⑦
⑧	⑧	⑧	⑧	⑧	⑧	⑧		⑧		⑧	Ⓘ	⑧	⑧	⑧	⑧	⑧	⑧	⑧	⑧	⑧
⑨	⑨	⑨	⑨	⑨	⑨	⑨		⑨		⑨	Ⓙ	⑨	⑨	⑨	⑨	⑨	⑨	⑨	⑨	⑨
											Ⓚ									
											Ⓛ									
											Ⓜ									
											Ⓝ									
											Ⓞ									
											Ⓟ									
											Ⓠ									
											Ⓡ									
											Ⓢ									
											Ⓣ									
											Ⓤ									
											Ⓥ									
											Ⓦ									
											Ⓧ									
											Ⓨ									
											Ⓩ									

＊注意：本答案紙限用 #2 (HB) 黑色鉛筆在「○」內塗黑、塗滿。

作答樣例：正　確　　錯　誤

聽　力　測　驗				
試題別				
試題冊號碼				

1 ⒶⒷⒸⒹ	11 ⒶⒷⒸⒹ	21 ⒶⒷⒸⒹ	31 ⒶⒷⒸⒹ	41 ⒶⒷⒸⒹ	51 ⒶⒷⒸⒹ
2 ⒶⒷⒸⒹ	12 ⒶⒷⒸⒹ	22 ⒶⒷⒸⒹ	32 ⒶⒷⒸⒹ	42 ⒶⒷⒸⒹ	52 ⒶⒷⒸⒹ
3 ⒶⒷⒸⒹ	13 ⒶⒷⒸⒹ	23 ⒶⒷⒸⒹ	33 ⒶⒷⒸⒹ	43 ⒶⒷⒸⒹ	53 ⒶⒷⒸⒹ
4 ⒶⒷⒸⒹ	14 ⒶⒷⒸⒹ	24 ⒶⒷⒸⒹ	34 ⒶⒷⒸⒹ	44 ⒶⒷⒸⒹ	54 ⒶⒷⒸⒹ
5 ⒶⒷⒸⒹ	15 ⒶⒷⒸⒹ	25 ⒶⒷⒸⒹ	35 ⒶⒷⒸⒹ	45 ⒶⒷⒸⒹ	55 ⒶⒷⒸⒹ
6 ⒶⒷⒸⒹ	16 ⒶⒷⒸⒹ	26 ⒶⒷⒸⒹ	36 ⒶⒷⒸⒹ	46 ⒶⒷⒸⒹ	56 ⒶⒷⒸⒹ
7 ⒶⒷⒸⒹ	17 ⒶⒷⒸⒹ	27 ⒶⒷⒸⒹ	37 ⒶⒷⒸⒹ	47 ⒶⒷⒸⒹ	57 ⒶⒷⒸⒹ
8 ⒶⒷⒸⒹ	18 ⒶⒷⒸⒹ	28 ⒶⒷⒸⒹ	38 ⒶⒷⒸⒹ	48 ⒶⒷⒸⒹ	58 ⒶⒷⒸⒹ
9 ⒶⒷⒸⒹ	19 ⒶⒷⒸⒹ	29 ⒶⒷⒸⒹ	39 ⒶⒷⒸⒹ	49 ⒶⒷⒸⒹ	59 ⒶⒷⒸⒹ
10 ⒶⒷⒸⒹ	20 ⒶⒷⒸⒹ	30 ⒶⒷⒸⒹ	40 ⒶⒷⒸⒹ	50 ⒶⒷⒸⒹ	60 ⒶⒷⒸⒹ

English Listening Comprehension Test

Test Book No. 3

This listening comprehension test will test your ability to understand spoken English. In this test, each conversation, statement and question will be spoken JUST ONE TIME. They will not be written out for you. There are four parts to this test. Special instructions will be given to you at the beginning of each part.

Part A

In Part A, you will see several pictures in your test book. For each picture, you will be asked 1 to 3 questions. For each question, you will hear four possible answers. Choose the best answer according to what you see in the picture.

Example:

You will see:

You will hear: What is this?

A. This is a table.
B. This is a chair.
C. This is a watch.
D. This is a doll.

The best answer to the question "What is this?" is B: "This is a chair." Therefore, you should choose answer B.

A. Questions 1-2

B. Questions 3-4

C. Question 5

D. Questions 6-7

E. Questions 8-9

F. Question 10

G. Questions 11-12

H. Questions 13-15

Part B

In Part B, you will hear 15 questions. After you hear a question, read the four possible answers in your test book and decide which one is the best answer to the question you have heard.

Example:

You will hear: What does your father do?

You will read: A. He's 50 years old.
B. He's a teacher.
C. He's hungry.
D. He's in Los Angeles.

The best answer to the question "What does your father do?" is B: "He's a teacher." Therefore, you should choose answer B.

Please go to the next page. ⇨

16. A. Yes, he sometimes eats at his friend's house.
    B. No, he always does.
    C. Yes, he sometimes eats at home.
    D. No, he sometimes eats at a restaurant.

17. A. I'm sorry to hear that.
    B. All right.
    C. Because he is very busy.
    D. No, he can't.

18. A. You can take a city bus.
    B. That's a good idea.
    C. Give me a hand.
    D. That's too bad.

19. A. It's summer.
    B. It's Monday.
    C. It's hot.
    D. It's July 9.

20. A. Do you like seeing movies?
    B. So do I.
    C. Neither do I.
    D. I don't think so.

21. A. Don't give up now.
    B. Have a good time.
    C. No, I'm too tired.
    D. I can't find it.

22. A. Certainly not. I am glad to help you.
    B. Of course not. I am glad to.
    C. Of course. You are very kind.
    D. No, he can carry it by himself.

23. A. So am I.
    B. So do I.
    C. So did I.
    D. So I was.

24. A. It's up to you.
    B. Why not?
    C. Take it easy.
    D. That's a good idea.

25. A. That's too bad.
    B. I hope so.
    C. There's something special.
    D. I went to bed very late last night.

26. A. I am looking down in order to look for my dog.
    B. I got bad grades in my tests yesterday.
    C. I have no idea why you look so sad.
    D. I am waiting for a bus.

27. A. They don't understand.
    B. They were in the living room.
    C. They don't like instant soup.
    D. They are swimming.

28. A. Not at all. Thanks.
    B. I'd love to.
    C. What is it about ?
    D. Yes, we will.

29. A. He works very hard.
    B. Young children like watching TV.
    C. That doesn't surprise me.
    D. There's something wrong with my bike.

30. A. Really?
    B. That's not bad.
    C. I don't know.
    D. You are all right.

Part C

In Part C, you will hear 15 conversations between a man and a woman. After each conversation, you will hear a question about the conversation. After you hear the question, read the four possible answers in your test book and choose the best answer to the question you have heard.

Example:

You will hear: (Man) How do you go to school every day?
(Woman) Usually by bus. Sometimes by taxi.

TONE: How does the woman go to school?

You will read: A. She always goes to school on foot.
B. She usually takes a bike.
C. She takes either a bus or a taxi.
D. She usually goes to school by bus, never by taxi.

The best answer to the question "How does the woman go to school?" is C: "She takes either a bus or a taxi." Therefore, you should choose answer C.

Please go to the next page. ⇨

31. A. In an airplane.
    B. In a restaurant.
    C. In a stadium.
    D. In a movie theater.

32. A. Steve looks good in anything.
    B. He knew someone who looked like Steve.
    C. He wishes he had a jacket like Steve.
    D. Steve should get a new jacket.

33. A. Mr. Smith doesn't work there anymore.
    B. Mr. Smith has too much work.
    C. Mr. Smith is out of the building.
    D. Mr. Smith is in a meeting.

34. A. It will be easy.
    B. It was postponed.
    C. He feels lucky.
    D. He's not prepared.

35. A. He was cold.
    B. He was hot.
    C. The air was stale.
    D. The room was old.

36. A. Yesterday.
    B. Two days ago.
    C. Three days ago.
    D. Early last week.

37. A. That the woman come to the party.
    B. A date with Barbara.
    C. That the woman cook for the party.
    D. A present for Bill.

38. A. She is also a customer.
    B. The vase has already been sold.
    C. She is new in town.
    D. The vase is not for sale.

39. A. She should find someone who likes children.
    B. She should hire someone responsible and trustworthy.
    C. She should hire his son.
    D. She should hire his son's girlfriend.

40. A. At a buffet.
    B. At a restaurant.
    C. At someone's house.
    D. At a dinner party.

41. A. How Richard traveled.
    B. Where Richard went.
    C. If Richard will go.
    D. How much Richard spent.

42. A. He was held up in traffic.
    B. He had no way to get home.
    C. He was busy at the office.
    D. His car had to be repaired.

43. A. The man can find work in the library.
    B. She can't help the man because she's working.
    C. She can work without air-conditioning.
    D. The man can do his work elsewhere.

44. A. The team played one hour longer yesterday.
    B. The team had better play one more game.
    C. The man should join a better team.
    D. The man's team is improving.

45. A. He looks like he's lost weight.
    B. He exercises regularly.
    C. He doesn't eat much.
    D. He told her so.

Part D

In Part D, you will hear 15 short talks. After each talk, you will hear a question about the talk. After you hear the question, read the four possible answers in your test book and choose the best answer to the question you have heard.

Example:

You will hear: Well, that's all for Unit 15. For today's homework, please do the review questions on page 80, and we'll check the answers tomorrow. Now, let's go on to Unit 16.

TONE: What is the teacher going to do next in today's class?

You will read: A. Check the homework.
B. Review Unit 15.
C. Start a new unit.
D. Answer students' questions.

The best answer to the question "What is the teacher going to do next in today's class?" is C: "Start a new unit." Therefore, you should choose answer C.

Please go to the next page. ⇨

46. A. Once.
 B. Twice.
 C. Three times.
 D. Four times.

47. A. In the lobby.
 B. In the basement.
 C. On the 3rd floor.
 D. On the 4th floor.

48. A. On the bus.
 B. At an airport.
 C. On the plane.
 D. In front of a boarding gate.

49. A. Advisers.
 B. Medical operators.
 C. Travel agents.
 D. Doctors.

50. A. Washington State.
 B. The Pacific Ocean station.
 C. WXYW.
 D. Citizen's Bank.

51. A. Vice-president of the company.
 B. Director of the advertising division.
 C. Professor at a university.
 D. Manager of the company.

52. A. They fished and raised crops.
 B. They cared for the children and raised crops.
 C. They cared for the children and made clothing.
 D. They made clothing and raised animals.

53. A. They worked in sun and rain.
 B. They worked all the year round.
 C. They went out to work even in typhoons.
 D. They worked in all weathers.

54. A. Ten o'clock.
 B. One o'clock.
 C. One-thirty.
 D. Two o'clock.

55. A. Congress was willing to develop a telegraph system.
 B. Congress refused to appropriate money for the purpose.
 C. Congress assisted private corporations to develop the telegraph system.
 D. Congress believed the telegraph system was worthless.

56. A. Raising funds.
 B. Lifting the nation's cultural level.
 C. Establishing free schools.
 D. Training ministers.

57. A. Lack of nutrients.
 B. Snow and ice.
 C. Heat and drought.
 D. Old age.

58. A. Business leadership.
 B. Investment.
 C. History.
 D. Seminar.

59. A. To demonstrate the latest use of computer graphics.
 B. To discuss the possibility of an economic depression.
 C. To explain the workings of the brain.
 D. To dramatize a famous mystery story.

60. A. A driver who got a speeding ticket.
 B. A newspaper editor who wrote this article.
 C. An officer who is directing the crackdown.
 D. A visitor who is traveling.

中級英語聽力檢定測驗答案紙

中文姓名 ________________　　　　測驗日期：民國 _____ 年 _____ 月 _____ 日

1. 准考證號碼					2. 出生						3. 國民身分證統一編號									
					年(民國)		月		日											
請依序將每個數字在下欄塗黑																				
⓪①②③④⑤⑥⑦⑧⑨	⓪①②③④⑤⑥⑦⑧⑨	⓪①②③④⑤⑥⑦⑧⑨	⓪①②③④⑤⑥⑦⑧⑨	⓪①②③④⑤⑥⑦⑧⑨	⓪①②③④⑤⑥⑦⑧⑨	⓪①②③④⑤⑥⑦⑧⑨	⓪①	⓪①②③④⑤⑥⑦⑧⑨	⓪①②③	⓪①②③④⑤⑥⑦⑧⑨	ⒶⒷⒸⒹⒺⒻⒼⒽⒾⒿⓀⓁⓂⓃⓄⓅⓆⓇⓈⓉⓊⓋⓌⓍⓎⓏ	⓪①②③④⑤⑥⑦⑧⑨	⓪①②③④⑤⑥⑦⑧⑨	⓪①②③④⑤⑥⑦⑧⑨	⓪①②③④⑤⑥⑦⑧⑨	⓪①②③④⑤⑥⑦⑧⑨	⓪①②③④⑤⑥⑦⑧⑨	⓪①②③④⑤⑥⑦⑧⑨	⓪①②③④⑤⑥⑦⑧⑨	⓪①②③④⑤⑥⑦⑧⑨

＊注意：本答案紙限用 #2 (HB) 黑色鉛筆在「○」內塗黑、塗滿。

作答樣例：正確　ⒶⒷ●Ⓓ

錯誤　ⒶⒷⒸⒹ（打勾）　ⒶⒷⒸⒹ（打叉）　ⒶⒷⒸⒹ（圈塗）　ⒶⒷⒸⒹ（未塗滿）

聽力測驗				
試題別				
試題冊號碼				

1 ⒶⒷⒸⒹ	11 ⒶⒷⒸⒹ	21 ⒶⒷⒸⒹ	31 ⒶⒷⒸⒹ	41 ⒶⒷⒸⒹ	51 ⒶⒷⒸⒹ
2 ⒶⒷⒸⒹ	12 ⒶⒷⒸⒹ	22 ⒶⒷⒸⒹ	32 ⒶⒷⒸⒹ	42 ⒶⒷⒸⒹ	52 ⒶⒷⒸⒹ
3 ⒶⒷⒸⒹ	13 ⒶⒷⒸⒹ	23 ⒶⒷⒸⒹ	33 ⒶⒷⒸⒹ	43 ⒶⒷⒸⒹ	53 ⒶⒷⒸⒹ
4 ⒶⒷⒸⒹ	14 ⒶⒷⒸⒹ	24 ⒶⒷⒸⒹ	34 ⒶⒷⒸⒹ	44 ⒶⒷⒸⒹ	54 ⒶⒷⒸⒹ
5 ⒶⒷⒸⒹ	15 ⒶⒷⒸⒹ	25 ⒶⒷⒸⒹ	35 ⒶⒷⒸⒹ	45 ⒶⒷⒸⒹ	55 ⒶⒷⒸⒹ
6 ⒶⒷⒸⒹ	16 ⒶⒷⒸⒹ	26 ⒶⒷⒸⒹ	36 ⒶⒷⒸⒹ	46 ⒶⒷⒸⒹ	56 ⒶⒷⒸⒹ
7 ⒶⒷⒸⒹ	17 ⒶⒷⒸⒹ	27 ⒶⒷⒸⒹ	37 ⒶⒷⒸⒹ	47 ⒶⒷⒸⒹ	57 ⒶⒷⒸⒹ
8 ⒶⒷⒸⒹ	18 ⒶⒷⒸⒹ	28 ⒶⒷⒸⒹ	38 ⒶⒷⒸⒹ	48 ⒶⒷⒸⒹ	58 ⒶⒷⒸⒹ
9 ⒶⒷⒸⒹ	19 ⒶⒷⒸⒹ	29 ⒶⒷⒸⒹ	39 ⒶⒷⒸⒹ	49 ⒶⒷⒸⒹ	59 ⒶⒷⒸⒹ
10 ⒶⒷⒸⒹ	20 ⒶⒷⒸⒹ	30 ⒶⒷⒸⒹ	40 ⒶⒷⒸⒹ	50 ⒶⒷⒸⒹ	60 ⒶⒷⒸⒹ

English Listening Comprehension Test

Test Book No. 4

This listening comprehension test will test your ability to understand spoken English. In this test, each conversation, statement and question will be spoken JUST ONE TIME. They will not be written out for you. There are four parts to this test. Special instructions will be given to you at the beginning of each part.

Part A

In Part A, you will see several pictures in your test book. For each picture, you will be asked 1 to 3 questions. For each question, you will hear four possible answers. Choose the best answer according to what you see in the picture.

Example:

You will see:

You will hear: What is this?

A. This is a table.
B. This is a chair.
C. This is a watch.
D. This is a doll.

The best answer to the question "What is this?" is B: "This is a chair." Therefore, you should choose answer B.

A. Questions 1-3

D. Question 9

B. Questions 4-6

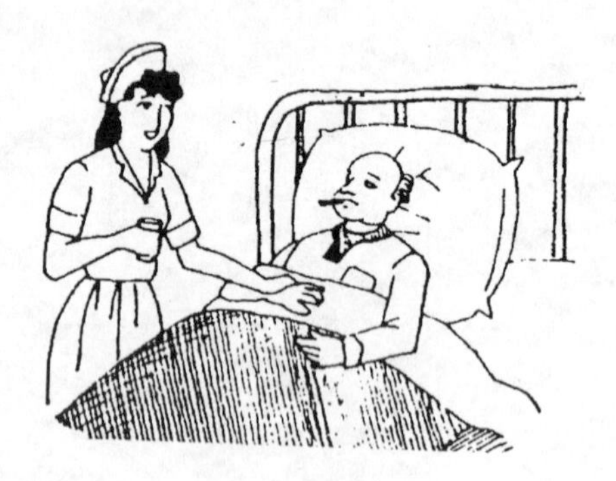

E. Questions 10-12

C. Questions 7-8

F. Questions 13-15

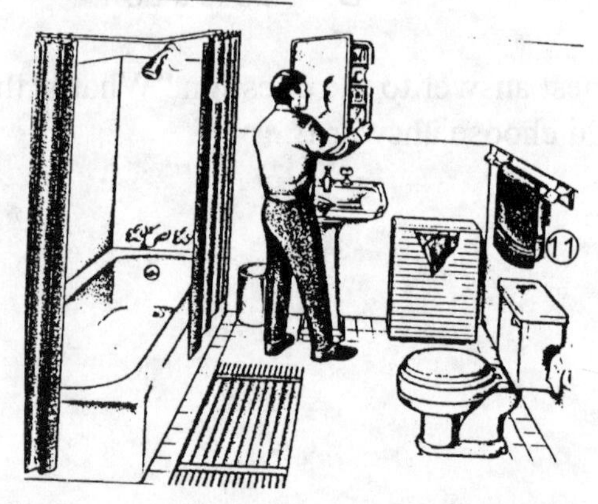

Part B

In Part B, you will hear 15 questions. After you hear a question, read the four possible answers in your test book and decide which one is the best answer to the question you have heard.

Example:

You will hear: What does your father do?

You will read: A. He's 50 years old.
B. He's a teacher.
C. He's hungry.
D. He's in Los Angeles.

The best answer to the question "What does your father do?" is B: "He's a teacher." Therefore, you should choose answer B.

Please go to the next page. ⇨

16. A. Yes, thank you.
    B. It is 5 dollars.
    C. We don't have any homework.
    D. I hope so.

17. A. Are you here?
    B. Let's go home.
    C. It always is.
    D. I stop it.

18. A. He doesn't run every day.
    B. He runs fast every day.
    C. He is too old to run.
    D. As fast as you.

19. A. His brother is, too.
    B. Neither does his brother.
    C. So is his brother.
    D. So does his brother.

20. A. It's very warm in winter.
    B. The weather is nice in winter.
    C. It's too cold in winter.
    D. No, they don't take a trip every winter.

21. A. How are you? Nice to see you again.
    B. Thank you. Glad to see you.
    C. How do you do? Nice to meet you.
    D. Have you eaten breakfast?

22. A. I bought a new car.
    B. By bus.
    C. I rode a bicycle.
    D. By studying.

23. A. Parking is never easy.
    B. There's no parking along this street.
    C. Look! Every car is gone!
    D. Because they liked to.

24. A. By car.
    B. Very quick.
    C. To Taipei.
    D. In a few minutes.

25. A. It must be Kevin.
    B. I would like to stay at home.
    C. I am so surprised.
    D. It doesn't interest me.

26. A. I'm interested in math.
    B. English is really an easy subject.
    C. I become excited about Chinese.
    D. I can't find a satisfying answer.

27. A. It won't write.
    B. Yes, I have a good pen.
    C. I don't need it.
    D. This is a new pen.

28. A. On Monday.
    B. It's Saturday.
    C. On Tuesday and Thursday.
    D. On Sunday morning.

29. A. Oh, that's too bad!
    B. Yes, it is.
    C. Have a good time!
    D. Of course, they can.

30. A. It's too hot in winter.
    B. I love it.
    C. So far so good.
    D. That's all right.

Part C

In Part C, you will hear 15 conversations between a man and a woman. After each conversation, you will hear a question about the conversation. After you hear the question, read the four possible answers in your test book and choose the best answer to the question you have heard.

Example:

You will hear: (Man) How do you go to school every day?
(Woman) Usually by bus. Sometimes by taxi.

TONE: How does the woman go to school?

You will read:
A. She always goes to school on foot.
B. She usually takes a bike.
C. She takes either a bus or a taxi.
D. She usually goes to school by bus, never by taxi.

The best answer to the question "How does the woman go to school?" is C: "She takes either a bus or a taxi." Therefore, you should choose answer C.

Please go to the next page. ⇨

31. A. He always eats more than he can.
    B. He eats while studying and working.
    C. He got sick because he ate too much.
    D. He is trying to study and work too much.

32. A. His tonsils are swollen.
    B. He doesn't feel well because he drank too much.
    C. He has trouble breathing after jogging.
    D. He has no appetite because he caught a cold.

33. A. At a zoo.
    B. At a museum.
    C. In a college cafeteria.
    D. At a bird house.

34. A. He is impudent.
    B. He is courageous.
    C. He is nervous.
    D. He is intelligent.

35. A. Because something was wrong with the lights.
    B. Because the electricity failed.
    C. Because the engineer made an error.
    D. Because the woman hadn't paid the electric bills for months.

36. A. Went to see the movie.
    B. Fell asleep.
    C. Played football.
    D. Watched the late movie.

37. A. He spilled coffee and discolored his shirt.
    B. He broke a coffee cup.
    C. He can't find an encyclopedia.
    D. He discolored the shirt with dirt.

38. A. The number of the publication.
    B. The name of the bookstore.
    C. The title of the book which will be most popular.
    D. The publisher's name.

39. A. It is too late for the woman to get a ticket.
    B. The woman must change her destination.
    C. The woman should wait until tomorrow.
    D. She will never be able to get a ticket.

40. A. The man must have been mistaken.
    B. It has been a long time since she went to see the show.
    C. Peter couldn't have been that old.
    D. Peter must be old because it has been years since she saw him.

41. A. Type the report.
    B. Write a report.
    C. Type the proposals.
    D. Attend the meeting.

42. A. Writing a research paper is a pain for her.
    B. She has a class at three o'clock.
    C. She hopes that she doesn't have to write a paper.
    D. She doesn't want to trouble him.

43. A. She can get two dresses and a pair of socks for 24 dollars.
    B. She shouldn't buy the dress because it's not a bargain.
    C. She can have free socks if she pays him 12 dollars for the dress.
    D. She will earn twelve dollars by selling socks.

44. A. He will take a sports class.
    B. He will pick up jogging.
    C. He will pursue athletics.
    D. He will go for his athletics teacher.

45. A. The restaurant was entirely destroyed by fire.
    B. The restaurant was open last July.
    C. The restaurant went bankrupt.
    D. The restaurant has been in the black since July.

Part D

In Part D, you will hear 15 short talks. After each talk, you will hear a question about the talk. After you hear the question, read the four possible answers in your test book and choose the best answer to the question you have heard.

Example:

You will hear: Well, that's all for Unit 15. For today's homework, please do the review questions on page 80, and we'll check the answers tomorrow. Now, let's go on to Unit 16.

TONE: What is the teacher going to do next in today's class?

You will read:
A. Check the homework.
B. Review Unit 15.
C. Start a new unit.
D. Answer students' questions.

The best answer to the question "What is the teacher going to do next in today's class?" is C: "Start a new unit." Therefore, you should choose answer C.

Please go to the next page. ⇨

46. A. Learned to do paper sculpture.
B. Designed and built houses.
C. Worked on drawing house plans.
D. Given talks about famous architects.

47. A. Humorous.
B. Tragic.
C. Sad.
D. Dark.

48. A. At the main entrance.
B. In the gift shop.
C. From the shopkeeper.
D. At the primate center.

49. A. The treatment of burns.
B. The process of conscious thought.
C. The body's ability to heal itself.
D. The body's unconscious reactions.

50. A. Basketball.
B. Soccer.
C. Table tennis.
D. Baseball.

51. A. He went rabbit hunting.
B. He was attacked by a rabbit.
C. He went fishing.
D. He went jogging.

52. A. Learning English.
B. Learning conversation skills.
C. Learning about foreign places.
D. Learning a foreign language.

53. A. Cowboys.
B. Frontiersmen.
C. Indians.
D. Film makers.

54. A. On a bus.
B. In a taxi.
C. On an airplane.
D. On the mass rapid transit system.

55. A. A customer.
B. A boss.
C. A teacher.
D. An operator.

56. A. A TV sports announcer.
B. A bike salesman.
C. A facility manager.
D. A teacher.

57. A. Soup.
B. Beer.
C. Bread.
D. Soft drink.

58. A. At a history lecture.
B. At a company which buys insurance.
C. At a meeting of employees.
D. At a birthday party.

59. A. A trip to Taipei.
B. The number of employees.
C. The name of a restaurant.
D. The charges of rooms.

60. A. The woman's wealth.
B. A note from a church.
C. Where the woman lived.
D. The woman's age.

中級英語聽力檢定測驗答案紙

中文姓名 ____________________　　測驗日期：民國 _____ 年 _____ 月 _____ 日

1. 准考證號碼					2. 出生						3. 國民身分證統一編號									
					年(民國)		月		日											
請依序將每個數字在下欄塗黑																				
⓪①②③④⑤⑥⑦⑧⑨	⓪①②③④⑤⑥⑦⑧⑨	⓪①②③④⑤⑥⑦⑧⑨	⓪①②③④⑤⑥⑦⑧⑨	⓪①②③④⑤⑥⑦⑧⑨	⓪①②③④⑤⑥⑦⑧⑨	⓪①②③④⑤⑥⑦⑧⑨	⓪①	⓪①②③④⑤⑥⑦⑧⑨	⓪①②③	⓪①②③④⑤⑥⑦⑧⑨	ⒶⒷⒸⒹⒺⒻⒼⒽⒾⒿⓀⓁⓂⓃⓄⓅⓆⓇⓈⓉⓊⓋⓌⓍⓎⓏ	⓪①②③④⑤⑥⑦⑧⑨	⓪①②③④⑤⑥⑦⑧⑨	⓪①②③④⑤⑥⑦⑧⑨	⓪①②③④⑤⑥⑦⑧⑨	⓪①②③④⑤⑥⑦⑧⑨	⓪①②③④⑤⑥⑦⑧⑨	⓪①②③④⑤⑥⑦⑧⑨	⓪①②③④⑤⑥⑦⑧⑨	⓪①②③④⑤⑥⑦⑧⑨

＊注意：本答案紙限用 #2 (HB) 黑色鉛筆在「○」內塗黑、塗滿。

作答樣例：正確　ⒶⒷ●Ⓓ

錯誤　ⒶⒷⒸⒹ　ⒶⒷⒸⒹ　ⒶⒷⒸⒹ　ⒶⒷⒸⒹ

聽力測驗				
試題別				
試題冊號碼				

1 ⒶⒷⒸⒹ	11 ⒶⒷⒸⒹ	21 ⒶⒷⒸⒹ	31 ⒶⒷⒸⒹ	41 ⒶⒷⒸⒹ	51 ⒶⒷⒸⒹ
2 ⒶⒷⒸⒹ	12 ⒶⒷⒸⒹ	22 ⒶⒷⒸⒹ	32 ⒶⒷⒸⒹ	42 ⒶⒷⒸⒹ	52 ⒶⒷⒸⒹ
3 ⒶⒷⒸⒹ	13 ⒶⒷⒸⒹ	23 ⒶⒷⒸⒹ	33 ⒶⒷⒸⒹ	43 ⒶⒷⒸⒹ	53 ⒶⒷⒸⒹ
4 ⒶⒷⒸⒹ	14 ⒶⒷⒸⒹ	24 ⒶⒷⒸⒹ	34 ⒶⒷⒸⒹ	44 ⒶⒷⒸⒹ	54 ⒶⒷⒸⒹ
5 ⒶⒷⒸⒹ	15 ⒶⒷⒸⒹ	25 ⒶⒷⒸⒹ	35 ⒶⒷⒸⒹ	45 ⒶⒷⒸⒹ	55 ⒶⒷⒸⒹ
6 ⒶⒷⒸⒹ	16 ⒶⒷⒸⒹ	26 ⒶⒷⒸⒹ	36 ⒶⒷⒸⒹ	46 ⒶⒷⒸⒹ	56 ⒶⒷⒸⒹ
7 ⒶⒷⒸⒹ	17 ⒶⒷⒸⒹ	27 ⒶⒷⒸⒹ	37 ⒶⒷⒸⒹ	47 ⒶⒷⒸⒹ	57 ⒶⒷⒸⒹ
8 ⒶⒷⒸⒹ	18 ⒶⒷⒸⒹ	28 ⒶⒷⒸⒹ	38 ⒶⒷⒸⒹ	48 ⒶⒷⒸⒹ	58 ⒶⒷⒸⒹ
9 ⒶⒷⒸⒹ	19 ⒶⒷⒸⒹ	29 ⒶⒷⒸⒹ	39 ⒶⒷⒸⒹ	49 ⒶⒷⒸⒹ	59 ⒶⒷⒸⒹ
10 ⒶⒷⒸⒹ	20 ⒶⒷⒸⒹ	30 ⒶⒷⒸⒹ	40 ⒶⒷⒸⒹ	50 ⒶⒷⒸⒹ	60 ⒶⒷⒸⒹ

English Listening Comprehension Test

Test Book No. 5

This listening comprehension test will test your ability to understand spoken English. In this test, each conversation, statement and question will be spoken JUST ONE TIME. They will not be written out for you. There are four parts to this test. Special instructions will be given to you at the beginning of each part.

Part A

In Part A, you will see several pictures in your test book. For each picture, you will be asked 1 to 3 questions. For each question, you will hear four possible answers. Choose the best answer according to what you see in the picture.

Example:

You will see:

You will hear: What is this?

A. This is a table.
B. This is a chair.
C. This is a watch.
D. This is a doll.

The best answer to the question "What is this?" is B: "This is a chair." Therefore, you should choose answer B.

A. Questions 1-3

D. Questions 10-12

B. Questions 4-6

E. Question 13-15

C. Questions 7-9

Part B

In Part B, you will hear 15 questions. After you hear a question, read the four possible answers in your test book and decide which one is the best answer to the question you have heard.

Example:

You will hear: What does your father do?

You will read: A. He's 50 years old.
B. He's a teacher.
C. He's hungry.
D. He's in Los Angeles.

The best answer to the question "What does your father do?" is B: "He's a teacher." Therefore, you should choose answer B.

Please go to the next page. ⇨

16. A. Very good.
    B. d-o-g—dog
    C. dog
    D. How are you?

17. A. For six hours.
    B. At six o'clock.
    C. Quite often.
    D. Yes, I do.

18. A. She walks to school.
    B. Yes, she walks to school.
    C. She doesn't walk to school.
    D. She goes to school every morning.

19. A. Very much.
    B. Those presents are very beautiful.
    C. They bought those presents at the store.
    D. No, they don't like those presents a lot.

20. A. I can't wait!
    B. I can't believe it!
    C. Oh, aren't they?
    D. Oh, I love it.

21. A. I have everything we'll need for camping.
    B. Where are the birds?
    C. I thought you brought the food.
    D. I'm sorry. I have an English test tomorrow.

22. A. You are welcome.
    B. Can I give you a hand?
    C. Camping at the lake can be exciting.
    D. I lost my car keys.

23. A. A little won't make you fat.
    B. Yes, I do.
    C. That's all right.
    D. No, thanks. I'm afraid of getting fat.

24. A. Please go to the next street.
    B. Every five minutes.
    C. You have to buy a ticket first.
    D. It is five dollars.

25. A. He often helps people.
    B. He is not lazy.
    C. I don't think so.
    D. I don't play with him.

26. A. I am glad to hear that.
    B. That's all right.
    C. He goes to the movies.
    D. He can play soccer.

27. A. I have no money.
    B. Oh, I don't know yet.
    C. I have two tickets.
    D. Can you go with me?

28. A. Yes, I can't.
    B. Neither do I.
    C. I want size 44.
    D. I can, too.

29. A. She accepts our idea now.
    B. I can't wait.
    C. You can tell her about this.
    D. She is kind to us.

30. A. Yes, I don't want to buy anything.
    B. I am sorry to trouble you.
    C. Yes, how much is this blue sweater?
    D. Of course, I'll give you a hand.

Part C

In Part C, you will hear 15 conversations between a man and a woman. After each conversation, you will hear a question about the conversation. After you hear the question, read the four possible answers in your test book and choose the best answer to the question you have heard.

Example:

You will hear: (Man) How do you go to school every day?
(Woman) Usually by bus. Sometimes by taxi.

TONE: How does the woman go to school?

You will read: A. She always goes to school on foot.
B. She usually takes a bike.
C. She takes either a bus or a taxi.
D. She usually goes to school by bus, never by taxi.

The best answer to the question "How does the woman go to school?" is C: "She takes either a bus or a taxi." Therefore, you should choose answer C.

Please go to the next page.

31. A. The snow storm in Michigan.
    B. The winter weather in the midwest.
    C. Departure of the flight.
    D. Delay of the airplane.

32. A. He is an undergraduate student.
    B. He studies mechanical engineering.
    C. He is majoring in electrical engineering.
    D. He is living in Mexico.

33. A. He would like to help the woman typing.
    B. He wonders how much he should pay her.
    C. He wants the woman to help him.
    D. He prefers to type the paper by himself.

34. A. Tomorrow will be fine.
    B. He is very upset.
    C. It's going to be icy tomorrow.
    D. The sky is going to be cloudy.

35. A. The woman needs the recipe which explains the amount of butter.
    B. He is reminding the woman to buy butter.
    C. This recipe requires two spoonfuls of butter.
    D. He doesn't want the woman to use a lot of butter.

36. A. He saw a beauty queen in Paris.
    B. Each city presents a queen for the beauty pageant.
    C. There are many beautiful ladies in Paris.
    D. Paris is the most attractive city of all.

37. A. Most of the students are majoring in statistics.
    B. Statistics is an elective course for freshmen.
    C. All economics majors must take statistics.
    D. Students can elect either mathematics or statistics.

38. A. He is pleased to know she enjoys jogging.
    B. The car runs really well.
    C. It has been ten years since he bought the car.
    D. The car usually starts with a little trouble.

39. A. She was very frightened.
    B. She had a heart problem.
    C. She lost the race.
    D. Overall, she was happy.

40. A. Read geography I for tomorrow.
    B. Read the second chapter for tomorrow.
    C. Read Chapter One for tomorrow.
    D. Read two chapters for tomorrow.

41. A. Turn down the radio.
    B. Turn off the radio.
    C. Keep the radio on.
    D. Change the radio station.

42. A. Hand the book to John.
    B. Give a math lesson to John.
    C. Ask John some math questions.
    D. Help John with his math assignment.

43. A. Keep his weight as it is.
    B. Pay attention to what she eats.
    C. Eat food which has more calories.
    D. Not to eat desserts after meals.

44. A. We have to learn how to repair computers.
    B. Using a computer requires a lot of knowledge.
    C. We cannot let computers control us.
    D. We should live without depending upon the computer.

45. A. She can manage much more.
    B. She will take one.
    C. She doesn't care how many she gets.
    D. She will not take any.

Part D

In Part D, you will hear 15 short talks. After each talk, you will hear a question about the talk. After you hear the question, read the four possible answers in your test book and choose the best answer to the question you have heard.

Example:

You will hear: Well, that's all for Unit 15. For today's homework, please do the review questions on page 80, and we'll check the answers tomorrow. Now, let's go on to Unit 16.

TONE: What is the teacher going to do next in today's class?

You will read:
A. Check the homework.
B. Review Unit 15.
C. Start a new unit.
D. Answer students' questions.

The best answer to the question "What is the teacher going to do next in today's class?" is C: "Start a new unit." Therefore, you should choose answer C.

Please go to the next page. ⇨

46. A. Spain.
    B. France.
    C. The Royal Hospital.
    D. Paris.

47. A. A referee.
    B. A sports announcer.
    C. A coach.
    D. A student.

48. A. Music.
    B. Literature.
    C. Dance.
    D. Painting.

49. A. Salad.
    B. Soup.
    C. Dinner.
    D. Dessert.

50. A. A lower unemployment rate.
    B. A new television program.
    C. A redevelopment project.
    D. A construction contract.

51. A. An essay.
    B. A magazine article.
    C. A poem.
    D. A short story.

52. A. The stage.
    B. London.
    C. England.
    D. The cinema.

53. A. In the park.
    B. By a famous landmark.
    C. In the museum dining room.
    D. Near the docks.

54. A. Pick up the phone right away.
    B. Take your seat immediately.
    C. Apply as soon as you can.
    D. Pay next month.

55. A. Many coats were lost.
    B. Some people forgot their tags.
    C. Many coats were destroyed.
    D. A confusing system was used.

56. A. To conserve energy.
    B. To save water.
    C. To report consumer fraud.
    D. To lock their doors.

57. A. A recording.
    B. A directory.
    C. A caller.
    D. A student.

58. A. Rent equipment.
    B. Sweep the ice.
    C. Buy jackets.
    D. Leave the arena.

59. A. Individuals can help very little.
    B. Recycling newspapers and glass is the answer.
    C. Economists must participate.
    D. Everyone should help.

60. A. There are many small farms.
    B. Only university graduates can become farmers.
    C. Farming is not a popular subject in school.
    D. Farming is a big business.

中級英語聽力檢定測驗答案紙

中文姓名 ____________________　　　測驗日期：民國 _____ 年 _____ 月 _____ 日

1. 准考證號碼					2. 出生 年(民國)		月		日		3. 國民身分證統一編號									
請依序將每個數字在下欄塗黑																				
⓪	⓪	⓪	⓪	⓪	⓪	⓪	⓪	⓪	⓪	⓪	Ⓐ	⓪	⓪	⓪	⓪	⓪	⓪	⓪	⓪	⓪
①	①	①	①	①	①	①	①	①	①	①	Ⓑ	①	①	①	①	①	①	①	①	①
②	②	②	②	②	②	②		②	②	②	Ⓒ	②	②	②	②	②	②	②	②	②
③	③	③	③	③	③	③		③	③	③	Ⓓ	③	③	③	③	③	③	③	③	③
④	④	④	④	④	④	④		④		④	Ⓔ	④	④	④	④	④	④	④	④	④
⑤	⑤	⑤	⑤	⑤	⑤	⑤		⑤		⑤	Ⓕ	⑤	⑤	⑤	⑤	⑤	⑤	⑤	⑤	⑤
⑥	⑥	⑥	⑥	⑥	⑥	⑥		⑥		⑥	Ⓖ	⑥	⑥	⑥	⑥	⑥	⑥	⑥	⑥	⑥
⑦	⑦	⑦	⑦	⑦	⑦	⑦		⑦		⑦	Ⓗ	⑦	⑦	⑦	⑦	⑦	⑦	⑦	⑦	⑦
⑧	⑧	⑧	⑧	⑧	⑧	⑧		⑧		⑧	Ⓘ	⑧	⑧	⑧	⑧	⑧	⑧	⑧	⑧	⑧
⑨	⑨	⑨	⑨	⑨	⑨	⑨		⑨		⑨	Ⓙ	⑨	⑨	⑨	⑨	⑨	⑨	⑨	⑨	⑨
											Ⓚ									
											Ⓛ									
											Ⓜ									
											Ⓝ									
											Ⓞ									
											Ⓟ									
											Ⓠ									
											Ⓡ									
											Ⓢ									
											Ⓣ									
											Ⓤ									
											Ⓥ									
											Ⓦ									
											Ⓧ									
											Ⓨ									
											Ⓩ									

＊注意：本答案紙限用 #2 (HB) 黑色鉛筆在「○」內塗黑、塗滿。

作答樣例：

正　確	錯　誤
ⒶⒷ●Ⓓ	ⒶⒷ✓Ⓓ
	ⒶⒷ✗Ⓓ
	ⒶⒷ○Ⓓ
	ⒶⒷ◐Ⓓ

聽　力　測　驗				
試題別				
試題冊號碼				

1 ⒶⒷⒸⒹ	11 ⒶⒷⒸⒹ	21 ⒶⒷⒸⒹ	31 ⒶⒷⒸⒹ	41 ⒶⒷⒸⒹ	51 ⒶⒷⒸⒹ
2 ⒶⒷⒸⒹ	12 ⒶⒷⒸⒹ	22 ⒶⒷⒸⒹ	32 ⒶⒷⒸⒹ	42 ⒶⒷⒸⒹ	52 ⒶⒷⒸⒹ
3 ⒶⒷⒸⒹ	13 ⒶⒷⒸⒹ	23 ⒶⒷⒸⒹ	33 ⒶⒷⒸⒹ	43 ⒶⒷⒸⒹ	53 ⒶⒷⒸⒹ
4 ⒶⒷⒸⒹ	14 ⒶⒷⒸⒹ	24 ⒶⒷⒸⒹ	34 ⒶⒷⒸⒹ	44 ⒶⒷⒸⒹ	54 ⒶⒷⒸⒹ
5 ⒶⒷⒸⒹ	15 ⒶⒷⒸⒹ	25 ⒶⒷⒸⒹ	35 ⒶⒷⒸⒹ	45 ⒶⒷⒸⒹ	55 ⒶⒷⒸⒹ
6 ⒶⒷⒸⒹ	16 ⒶⒷⒸⒹ	26 ⒶⒷⒸⒹ	36 ⒶⒷⒸⒹ	46 ⒶⒷⒸⒹ	56 ⒶⒷⒸⒹ
7 ⒶⒷⒸⒹ	17 ⒶⒷⒸⒹ	27 ⒶⒷⒸⒹ	37 ⒶⒷⒸⒹ	47 ⒶⒷⒸⒹ	57 ⒶⒷⒸⒹ
8 ⒶⒷⒸⒹ	18 ⒶⒷⒸⒹ	28 ⒶⒷⒸⒹ	38 ⒶⒷⒸⒹ	48 ⒶⒷⒸⒹ	58 ⒶⒷⒸⒹ
9 ⒶⒷⒸⒹ	19 ⒶⒷⒸⒹ	29 ⒶⒷⒸⒹ	39 ⒶⒷⒸⒹ	49 ⒶⒷⒸⒹ	59 ⒶⒷⒸⒹ
10 ⒶⒷⒸⒹ	20 ⒶⒷⒸⒹ	30 ⒶⒷⒸⒹ	40 ⒶⒷⒸⒹ	50 ⒶⒷⒸⒹ	60 ⒶⒷⒸⒹ

English Listening Comprehension Test

Test Book No.6

This listening comprehension test will test your ability to understand spoken English. In this test, each conversation, statement and question will be spoken JUST ONE TIME. They will not be written out for you. There are four parts to this test. Special instructions will be given to you at the beginning of each part.

Part A

In Part A, you will see several pictures in your test book. For each picture, you will be asked 1 to 3 questions. For each question, you will hear four possible answers. Choose the best answer according to what you see in the picture.

Example:

You will see:

You will hear: What is this?

A. This is a table.
B. This is a chair.
C. This is a watch.
D. This is a doll.

The best answer to the question "What is this?" is B: "This is a chair." Therefore, you should choose answer B.

A. Questions 1-3

B. Questions 4-6

C. Questions 7-9

D. Questions 10-12

E. Questions 13-14

F. Question 15

Part B

In Part B, you will hear 15 questions. After you hear a question, read the four possible answers in your test book and decide which one is the best answer to the question you have heard.

Example:

You will hear: What does your father do?

You will read: A. He's 50 years old.
B. He's a teacher.
C. He's hungry.
D. He's in Los Angeles.

The best answer to the question "What does your father do?" is B: "He's a teacher." Therefore, you should choose answer B.

Please go to the next page. ⇨

16. A. Why do you come to me?
    B. I know you will come.
    C. That's your problem.
    D. What's the matter?

17. A. So am I.
    B. It is your night.
    C. It's not mine, either.
    D. I don't like your day.

18. A. I think it looks like medicine.
    B. It tastes delicious.
    C. I taste it carefully.
    D. Yes, it's very good.

19. A. Yes, I am.
    B. No, I'm not playing.
    C. Yes, we're watching TV.
    D. No, we're playing.

20. A. Yes, I never.
    B. Of course, I don't.
    C. Sure, I do.
    D. Why? I don't, either.

21. A. I don't, either.
    B. Mind your own business.
    C. That's not a good habit.
    D. Can you give me a hand?

22. A. It's late.
    B. It leaves at 3:00.
    C. I'll see you then.
    D. It takes a lot of time.

23. A. I'd love to.
    B. I can't believe it.
    C. Why not me?
    D. Certainly, I wouldn't.

24. A. Fine, how do you do?
    B. Fine, nice to know you, John.
    C. Oh, fine, it is kind of you.
    D. I am fine. Thank you. How are you?

25. A. Yes, it's English.
    B. No, the second class.
    C. No, you're right.
    D. Yes, I speak good Chinese.

26. A. Not the television.
    B. The sofas are.
    C. They are chairs.
    D. It's not a desk.

27. A. It is hot in summer.
    B. It is summer.
    C. It's Sunday.
    D. I like summer very much.

28. A. Yes, there is.
    B. Yes, there is not.
    C. Please turn off the light.
    D. I do not mean it.

29. A. Everything was on sale.
    B. We didn't even sell a bun.
    C. We didn't have to pay anything.
    D. Our boss thought much about our customers.

30. A. We can't wait!
    B. That's too bad.
    C. Really? Why did they buy another TV?
    D. I wish it's ours.

Part C

In Part C, you will hear 15 conversations between a man and a woman. After each conversation, you will hear a question about the conversation. After you hear the question, read the four possible answers in your test book and choose the best answer to the question you have heard.

Example:

You will hear: (Man) How do you go to school every day?
(Woman) Usually by bus. Sometimes by taxi.

TONE: How does the woman go to school?

You will read:
A. She always goes to school on foot.
B. She usually takes a bike.
C. She takes either a bus or a taxi.
D. She usually goes to school by bus, never by taxi.

The best answer to the question "How does the woman go to school?" is C: "She takes either a bus or a taxi." Therefore, you should choose answer C.

Please go to the next page. ⇨

31. A. She should try on one or two sweaters.
    B. She must buy one or two sweaters.
    C. She should be ready to take two sweaters home.
    D. She should select one of the best sweaters.

32. A. She doesn't know how she is doing in French.
    B. Her four skills of French are highly improved.
    C. Her speaking ability is average.
    D. She can't manage the course as much as she wants to.

33. A. He doesn't know if Mr. Lee was born in Indonesia.
    B. He doesn't know where Mr. Lee lived before.
    C. He doesn't know when Mr. Lee will go to Hong Kong.
    D. He doesn't know where Mr. Lee grew up.

34. A. He wants the woman to borrow his book.
    B. He suggests that she find the book if she wants to borrow it.
    C. If she had found the book, she could have.
    D. He brought the book home, but it's disappeared.

35. A. He is folding his napkin.
    B. He is looking for his fork.
    C. He is eating food without a fork.
    D. He is becoming frustrated because he can't find his napkin.

36. A. He thinks she is an excellent teacher.
    B. The new teacher is obnoxious.
    C. There should be a better teacher than she.
    D. She is a very rude teacher.

37. A. To the movies.
    B. To the flower garden.
    C. To the concert.
    D. To the zoo.

38. A. Order a sofa this afternoon.
    B. Send a catalog of sofas.
    C. Deliver a sofa.
    D. Sit on a sofa.

39. A. He can't swing a golf club well.
    B. He hurt his back.
    C. He used to be a good golfer, but is not any more.
    D. He always has a backache.

40. A. Jason Daniels isn't home right now.
    B. The man dialed the wrong number.
    C. Jason Daniels can't come to the phone right now.
    D. Jason Daniels doesn't want to speak to the caller.

41. A. He is a coffee drinker.
    B. He likes to drink tea.
    C. He wants a coffee refill.
    D. Coffee makes him sick.

42. A. She feels that the man must go there by himself.
    B. She is complaining about standing in line and waiting.
    C. She is disappointed that the cafeteria is always crowded.
    D. She feels she should stand in line.

43. A. Everyone will enjoy the game today.
    B. It's nice weather.
    C. Tomorrow will be better weather.
    D. He expected better weather.

44. A. She feels that he should go on a diet.
    B. She thinks that he must become a vegetarian.
    C. She is surprised that he is not heavy.
    D. She is upset that he is overweight.

45. A. The beautiful scene that he has never seen before is breathtaking.
    B. The river appears to flow in the opposite direction.
    C. The river starts from a lake.
    D. The mountain range gives rise to many streams.

Part D

In Part D, you will hear 15 short talks. After each talk, you will hear a question about the talk. After you hear the question, read the four possible answers in your test book and choose the best answer to the question you have heard.

Example:

You will hear: Well, that's all for Unit 15. For today's homework, please do the review questions on page 80, and we'll check the answers tomorrow. Now, let's go on to Unit 16.

TONE: What is the teacher going to do next in today's class?

You will read:
A. Check the homework.
B. Review Unit 15.
C. Start a new unit.
D. Answer students' questions.

The best answer to the question "What is the teacher going to do next in today's class?" is C: "Start a new unit." Therefore, you should choose answer C.

Please go to the next page.

46. A. Donald Duck.
    B. Pluto.
    C. Snow White.
    D. Goofy.

47. A. For 15 minutes.
    B. For one hour.
    C. All night long.
    D. For two hours.

48. A. The tickets are all sold out.
    B. The ceiling of the theater is leaking.
    C. The movie is not very funny.
    D. The film has been misplaced.

49. A. A menu.
    B. A set-price dinner.
    C. A table.
    D. A dessert.

50. A. One day.
    B. Three days.
    C. Six days.
    D. Eleven days.

51. A. They make exciting writing.
    B. They help to sell papers.
    C. People hate to read these articles.
    D. UFOs are rare stories.

52. A. A pupil.
    B. A biology professor.
    C. An eye specialist.
    D. A safety expert.

53. A. 20.
    B. More than 20.
    C. Less than 20.
    D. 7.

54. A. To help Ms. Williamson find the Lost and Found Center.
    B. To tell Ms. Williamson that she has a telephone call.
    C. To bring Ms. Williamson to the Lost and Found Center.
    D. To report that Ms. Williamson is lost.

55. A. A flight schedule.
    B. Dinner in a restaurant.
    C. A train.
    D. A bus.

56. A. At a board of directors meeting.
    B. At a courier service counter.
    C. At a contract signing ceremony.
    D. At a funeral ceremony.

57. A. A newspaper.
    B. A radio station.
    C. A telephone company.
    D. A magazine.

58. A. He is trying to make a serious proposal.
    B. He is trying to ask for information.
    C. He is trying to amuse the audience.
    D. He is trying to warn the audience.

59. A. Consumers.
    B. Doctors.
    C. Farmers.
    D. Students.

60. A. To inform people of the zoo show.
    B. To announce the zoo will close soon.
    C. To advertise goods sold at the gift shop.
    D. To promote a restaurant serving lunch at the zoo.

中級英語聽力檢定測驗答案紙

中文姓名 ____________________　　　　測驗日期：民國 _____ 年 _____ 月 _____ 日

1. 准考證號碼					2. 出	生					3. 國民身分證統一編號									
					年(民國)		月		日											
請依序將每個數字在下欄塗黑																				
0	0	0	0	0	0	0	0	0	0	0	A	0	0	0	0	0	0	0	0	0
1	1	1	1	1	1	1	1	1	1	1	B	1	1	1	1	1	1	1	1	1
2	2	2	2	2	2	2		2	2	2	C	2	2	2	2	2	2	2	2	2
3	3	3	3	3	3	3		3	3	3	D	3	3	3	3	3	3	3	3	3
4	4	4	4	4	4	4		4		4	E	4	4	4	4	4	4	4	4	4
5	5	5	5	5	5	5		5		5	F	5	5	5	5	5	5	5	5	5
6	6	6	6	6	6	6		6		6	G	6	6	6	6	6	6	6	6	6
7	7	7	7	7	7	7		7		7	H	7	7	7	7	7	7	7	7	7
8	8	8	8	8	8	8		8		8	I	8	8	8	8	8	8	8	8	8
9	9	9	9	9	9	9		9		9	J	9	9	9	9	9	9	9	9	9
											K									
											L									
											M									
											N									
											O									
											P									
											Q									
											R									
											S									
											T									
											U									
											V									
											W									
											X									
											Y									
											Z									

＊注意：本答案紙限用 #2 (HB) 黑色鉛筆在「○」內塗黑、塗滿。

作答樣例：正　確　　錯　誤

A B ● D　　A B C D / A B C D / A B C D / A B C D

聽　力　測　驗				
試題別				
試題冊號碼				

1 A B C D	11 A B C D	21 A B C D	31 A B C D	41 A B C D	51 A B C D
2 A B C D	12 A B C D	22 A B C D	32 A B C D	42 A B C D	52 A B C D
3 A B C D	13 A B C D	23 A B C D	33 A B C D	43 A B C D	53 A B C D
4 A B C D	14 A B C D	24 A B C D	34 A B C D	44 A B C D	54 A B C D
5 A B C D	15 A B C D	25 A B C D	35 A B C D	45 A B C D	55 A B C D
6 A B C D	16 A B C D	26 A B C D	36 A B C D	46 A B C D	56 A B C D
7 A B C D	17 A B C D	27 A B C D	37 A B C D	47 A B C D	57 A B C D
8 A B C D	18 A B C D	28 A B C D	38 A B C D	48 A B C D	58 A B C D
9 A B C D	19 A B C D	29 A B C D	39 A B C D	49 A B C D	59 A B C D
10 A B C D	20 A B C D	30 A B C D	40 A B C D	50 A B C D	60 A B C D

English Listening Comprehension Test

Test Book No. 7

This listening comprehension test will test your ability to understand spoken English. In this test, each conversation, statement and question will be spoken JUST ONE TIME. They will not be written out for you. There are four parts to this test. Special instructions will be given to you at the beginning of each part.

Part A

In Part A, you will see several pictures in your test book. For each picture, you will be asked 1 to 3 questions. For each question, you will hear four possible answers. Choose the best answer according to what you see in the picture.

Example:

You will see:

You will hear: What is this?

A. This is a table.
B. This is a chair.
C. This is a watch.
D. This is a doll.

The best answer to the question "What is this?" is B: "This is a chair." Therefore, you should choose answer B.

A. Questions 1-2

B. Questions 3-5

C. Questions 6-8

D. Questions 9-10

E. Questions 11-12

F. Questions 13-15

Part B

In Part B, you will hear 15 questions. After you hear a question, read the four possible answers in your test book and decide which one is the best answer to the question you have heard.

Example:

<u>You will hear:</u> What does your father do?

<u>You will read:</u> A. He's 50 years old.
B. He's a teacher.
C. He's hungry.
D. He's in Los Angeles.

The best answer to the question "What does your father do?" is B: "He's a teacher." Therefore, you should choose answer B.

Please go to the next page. ⇨

16. A. That is a good idea.
    B. I have many swimsuits.
    C. I have no idea.
    D. When will you go?

17. A. I am sorry. He is not at home now.
    B. Who are you?
    C. Mr. Lin can speak good English.
    D. What do you mean?

18. A. He is in the living room.
    B. He is not in the room.
    C. He is watching TV.
    D. He is studying.

19. A. By bus.
    B. I liked it.
    C. I had a present.
    D. Many people were there.

20. A. Of course, but I can't.
    B. Yes, I have a math test.
    C. All right, you don't.
    D. Yes, I don't want to.

21. A. So did I.
    B. Neither did I.
    C. So I did.
    D. Neither I did.

22. A. That's okay.
    B. That's a good idea.
    C. What are you saying?
    D. No, I guess not.

23. A. Yes, I have. I have borrowed one.
    B. Yes, I do. I have borrowed one.
    C. Yes, you are. I have borrowed one.
    D. Yes, I have. I have lent one.

24. A. I have many neighbors.
    B. I am glad to meet you.
    C. My neighbors all live here.
    D. It sounds interesting.

25. A. She is a teacher.
    B. She is my aunt.
    C. She swims in the pool.
    D. She goes to the park every day.

26. A. A deal is a deal.
    B. So will you.
    C. What can I do?
    D. I hope so.

27. A. Yes, I didn't turn it on.
    B. No, and I'll turn it on yesterday.
    C. No, but I'll turn it on right away.
    D. Yes, I'll turn it on right away.

28. A. Yes, I'm right.
    B. Yes, something happened.
    C. No, I happened to something.
    D. No, there's something wrong with me.

29. A. Yesterday was a nice day.
    B. Yesterday was October 5.
    C. It rained yesterday.
    D. Yesterday was Thursday.

30. A. Yes, I did need help.
    B. No, you may.
    C. Yes, I want some shirts.
    D. Why?

Part C

In Part C, you will hear 15 conversations between a man and a woman. After each conversation, you will hear a question about the conversation. After you hear the question, read the four possible answers in your test book and choose the best answer to the question you have heard.

Example:

You will hear: (Man) How do you go to school every day?
(Woman) Usually by bus. Sometimes by taxi.

TONE: How does the woman go to school?

You will read: A. She always goes to school on foot.
B. She usually takes a bike.
C. She takes either a bus or a taxi.
D. She usually goes to school by bus, never by taxi.

The best answer to the question "How does the woman go to school?" is C: "She takes either a bus or a taxi." Therefore, you should choose answer C.

Please go to the next page. ⇨

31. A. Cleaning the house on Monday.
    B. Putting things away in his office on Monday.
    C. His health problem.
    D. The weather on Monday.

32. A. Where he can get a good car.
    B. How often he can travel by his car.
    C. How much he can sell his car for.
    D. Whether or not he can drive to California and come back.

33. A. He was tired.
    B. His appointment was changed.
    C. He had a flat tire.
    D. His bicycle was stolen.

34. A. Check-in counter at the airport.
    B. At the gate at the airport.
    C. In the air.
    D. At customs.

35. A. He will be ready for take off.
    B. He will be ready to board.
    C. He will arrive in Colorado.
    D. He will stow all luggage under the seat.

36. A. She is teaching a different subject.
    B. She was dismissed.
    C. She is changing jobs.
    D. She doesn't like teaching any more.

37. A. She's afraid of going out at night.
    B. She had to do some baking.
    C. She wanted to get ready for a plane trip.
    D. She was moving to a new apartment.

38. A. Shave.
    B. Finish with green paint.
    C. Move in here.
    D. Travel.

39. A. To see the Dean.
    B. To watch the team.
    C. To weigh herself.
    D. To give a demonstration.

40. A. Near an art gallery.
    B. In front of a library.
    C. At a stoplight.
    D. Outside a bookstore.

41. A. His change.
    B. Something to read.
    C. A different waitress.
    D. A copy of the order form.

42. A. Take his typewriter to the repair shop.
    B. Soundproof his room.
    C. Work in the basement.
    D. Listen for his roommate.

43. A. They work in the same department.
    B. They are distantly related.
    C. They are both doctors.
    D. They are both chemists.

44. A. He's better.
    B. He's complaining.
    C. He's sick in bed.
    D. He's cold.

45. A. Try on the jacket.
    B. Try on the suit.
    C. Continue looking.
    D. Buy a fur coat.

Part D

In Part D, you will hear 15 short talks. After each talk, you will hear a question about the talk. After you hear the question, read the four possible answers in your test book and choose the best answer to the question you have heard.

Example:

You will hear: Well, that's all for Unit 15. For today's homework, please do the review questions on page 80, and we'll check the answers tomorrow. Now, let's go on to Unit 16.

TONE: What is the teacher going to do next in today's class?

You will read:
A. Check the homework.
B. Review Unit 15.
C. Start a new unit.
D. Answer students' questions.

The best answer to the question "What is the teacher going to do next in today's class?" is C: "Start a new unit." Therefore, you should choose answer C.

Please go to the next page. ⇨

46. A. To demonstrate tutoring techniques.
    B. To explain school policies.
    C. To recruit workers.
    D. To explain a service.

47. A. He'll work at Silverlode.
    B. He'll fire Mr. Haskell.
    C. He'll ask Mr. Haskell again.
    D. He'll stay on as president.

48. A. Sunday.
    B. Tuesday.
    C. Friday.
    D. Saturday.

49. A. Five.
    B. Six.
    C. Seven.
    D. Eight.

50. A. Film and society.
    B. A film society.
    C. Rare films.
    D. How to make a film.

51. A. Synthetic materials.
    B. Masses of seaweed.
    C. Parts of vegetables.
    D. Parts of animals and fish.

52. A. A dog.
    B. A musical instrument.
    C. A ship.
    D. A horse.

53. A. Cartoons.
    B. The rural Mid-west.
    C. His father.
    D. Traveling around the world.

54. A. Stones.
    B. Hands.
    C. A hat.
    D. A scarf.

55. A. Experienced drivers.
    B. New drivers.
    C. Driving examiners.
    D. Movie-goers.

56. A. Discussing psychology.
    B. Introducing a speaker.
    C. Murdering someone.
    D. Solving a crime.

57. A. Question the offer.
    B. Reject the offer.
    C. Begin a strike.
    D. Accept the offer.

58. A. That the flight is boarding.
    B. That a caller is waiting.
    C. That Dr. Reed should make a phone call.
    D. That the line is busy.

59. A. A lower drinking age.
    B. Cutting cedar trees.
    C. Shortage of water.
    D. The cost of beer.

60. A. The date when the first exam will take place.
    B. The date when the school will begin.
    C. The date when the paper is due.
    D. The date when the instructor left.

中級英語聽力檢定測驗答案紙

中文姓名 ______________　　　　測驗日期：民國 _____ 年 _____ 月 _____ 日

1. 准考證號碼					2. 出生						3. 國民身分證統一編號									
					年（民國）		月		日											
請依序將每個數字在下欄塗黑																				
⓪	⓪	⓪	⓪	⓪	⓪	⓪	⓪	⓪	⓪	⓪	Ⓐ	⓪	⓪	⓪	⓪	⓪	⓪	⓪	⓪	⓪
①	①	①	①	①	①	①	①	①	①	①	Ⓑ	①	①	①	①	①	①	①	①	①
②	②	②	②	②	②	②		②	②	②	Ⓒ	②	②	②	②	②	②	②	②	②
③	③	③	③	③	③	③		③	③	③	Ⓓ	③	③	③	③	③	③	③	③	③
④	④	④	④	④	④	④		④		④	Ⓔ	④	④	④	④	④	④	④	④	④
⑤	⑤	⑤	⑤	⑤	⑤	⑤		⑤		⑤	Ⓕ	⑤	⑤	⑤	⑤	⑤	⑤	⑤	⑤	⑤
⑥	⑥	⑥	⑥	⑥	⑥	⑥		⑥		⑥	Ⓖ	⑥	⑥	⑥	⑥	⑥	⑥	⑥	⑥	⑥
⑦	⑦	⑦	⑦	⑦	⑦	⑦		⑦		⑦	Ⓗ	⑦	⑦	⑦	⑦	⑦	⑦	⑦	⑦	⑦
⑧	⑧	⑧	⑧	⑧	⑧	⑧		⑧		⑧	Ⓘ	⑧	⑧	⑧	⑧	⑧	⑧	⑧	⑧	⑧
⑨	⑨	⑨	⑨	⑨	⑨	⑨		⑨		⑨	Ⓙ	⑨	⑨	⑨	⑨	⑨	⑨	⑨	⑨	⑨
											Ⓚ									
											Ⓛ									
											Ⓜ									
											Ⓝ									
											Ⓞ									
											Ⓟ									
											Ⓠ									
											Ⓡ									
											Ⓢ									
											Ⓣ									
											Ⓤ									
											Ⓥ									
											Ⓦ									
											Ⓧ									
											Ⓨ									
											Ⓩ									

＊注意：本答案紙限用 #2 (HB) 黑色鉛筆在「○」內塗黑、塗滿。

作答樣例：

正　確	錯　誤
ⒶⒷ●Ⓓ	ⒶⒷⒸⒹ
	ⒶⒷⒸⒹ
	ⒶⒷⒸⒹ
	ⒶⒷⒸⒹ

聽　力　測　驗				
試題別				
試題冊號碼				

1 ⒶⒷⒸⒹ	11 ⒶⒷⒸⒹ	21 ⒶⒷⒸⒹ	31 ⒶⒷⒸⒹ	41 ⒶⒷⒸⒹ	51 ⒶⒷⒸⒹ
2 ⒶⒷⒸⒹ	12 ⒶⒷⒸⒹ	22 ⒶⒷⒸⒹ	32 ⒶⒷⒸⒹ	42 ⒶⒷⒸⒹ	52 ⒶⒷⒸⒹ
3 ⒶⒷⒸⒹ	13 ⒶⒷⒸⒹ	23 ⒶⒷⒸⒹ	33 ⒶⒷⒸⒹ	43 ⒶⒷⒸⒹ	53 ⒶⒷⒸⒹ
4 ⒶⒷⒸⒹ	14 ⒶⒷⒸⒹ	24 ⒶⒷⒸⒹ	34 ⒶⒷⒸⒹ	44 ⒶⒷⒸⒹ	54 ⒶⒷⒸⒹ
5 ⒶⒷⒸⒹ	15 ⒶⒷⒸⒹ	25 ⒶⒷⒸⒹ	35 ⒶⒷⒸⒹ	45 ⒶⒷⒸⒹ	55 ⒶⒷⒸⒹ
6 ⒶⒷⒸⒹ	16 ⒶⒷⒸⒹ	26 ⒶⒷⒸⒹ	36 ⒶⒷⒸⒹ	46 ⒶⒷⒸⒹ	56 ⒶⒷⒸⒹ
7 ⒶⒷⒸⒹ	17 ⒶⒷⒸⒹ	27 ⒶⒷⒸⒹ	37 ⒶⒷⒸⒹ	47 ⒶⒷⒸⒹ	57 ⒶⒷⒸⒹ
8 ⒶⒷⒸⒹ	18 ⒶⒷⒸⒹ	28 ⒶⒷⒸⒹ	38 ⒶⒷⒸⒹ	48 ⒶⒷⒸⒹ	58 ⒶⒷⒸⒹ
9 ⒶⒷⒸⒹ	19 ⒶⒷⒸⒹ	29 ⒶⒷⒸⒹ	39 ⒶⒷⒸⒹ	49 ⒶⒷⒸⒹ	59 ⒶⒷⒸⒹ
10 ⒶⒷⒸⒹ	20 ⒶⒷⒸⒹ	30 ⒶⒷⒸⒹ	40 ⒶⒷⒸⒹ	50 ⒶⒷⒸⒹ	60 ⒶⒷⒸⒹ

English Listening Comprehension Test

Test Book No. 8

This listening comprehension test will test your ability to understand spoken English. In this test, each conversation, statement and question will be spoken JUST ONE TIME. They will not be written out for you. There are four parts to this test. Special instructions will be given to you at the beginning of each part.

Part A

In Part A, you will see several pictures in your test book. For each picture, you will be asked 1 to 3 questions. For each question, you will hear four possible answers. Choose the best answer according to what you see in the picture.

Example:

You will see:

You will hear: What is this?

A. This is a table.
B. This is a chair.
C. This is a watch.
D. This is a doll.

The best answer to the question "What is this?" is B: "This is a chair." Therefore, you should choose answer B.

A. Questions 1-3

D. Questions 9-10

B. Questions 4-5

E. Questions 11-13

C. Questions 6-8

F. Questions 14-15

Part B

In Part B, you will hear 15 questions. After you hear a question, read the four possible answers in your test book and decide which one is the best answer to the question you have heard.

Example:

You will hear: What does your father do?

You will read:
A. He's 50 years old.
B. He's a teacher.
C. He's hungry.
D. He's in Los Angeles.

The best answer to the question "What does your father do?" is B: "He's a teacher." Therefore, you should choose answer B.

Please go to the next page. ⇨

16. A. Very near from here.
    B. About four hours.
    C. You can go there by train.
    D. I think you will be lost.

17. A. Yes, I don't want to go.
    B. No, I have a test in English tomorrow.
    C. Yes, I prefer to stay at home.
    D. No, I'd like to.

18. A. Their prices are reasonable for the quantity.
    B. They stopped giving money to customers.
    C. Your money isn't worth as much as before.
    D. I will sell it if the price is right.

19. A. Sure, here you are.
    B. Sure, here are you.
    C. Of course, here is it.
    D. Of course. You are here.

20. A. I'm sorry he's not home.
    B. I'm Mrs. Wang. Who are you?
    C. Where are you calling from?
    D. It's me. What's wrong?

21. A. Once a week.
    B. I like to study.
    C. I always go by bike.
    D. I leave my house at seven.

22. A. A table for two, please.
    B. Don't worry. It won't break easily.
    C. Great. I am really hungry.
    D. Can you fish?

23. A. Stand up, please.
    B. I can't go hiking with my classmate.
    C. Cheer up, Tom.
    D. It's very nice of you.

24. A. There are desks in the classroom.
    B. There are forty-five desks in it.
    C. There are many chairs in the classroom.
    D. There are many desks in it.

25. A. Sweet-and-sour pork tastes delicious.
    B. I've never tasted sweet-and-sour chicken.
    C. I also bought some vegetables.
    D. Meat was too expensive today.

26. A. It is John.
    B. It isn't me.
    C. Mary did.
    D. My younger brother does.

27. A. Yes, it is. It's hers.
    B. No, it isn't. It's mine.
    C. Yes, they are. They're hers.
    D. No, they aren't. They aren't mine.

28. A. Maybe you are right.
    B. Yes, I hate noise.
    C. Yes, it's so exciting.
    D. No, people in big cities are friendly.

29. A. I don't see it.
    B. It is very hard to learn.
    C. I don't know.
    D. This road is a nice road.

30. A. I am going to America.
    B. You would know that if you asked me.
    C. I lived here last year.
    D. I have been to California.

Part C

In Part C, you will hear 15 conversations between a man and a woman. After each conversation, you will hear a question about the conversation. After you hear the question, read the four possible answers in your test book and choose the best answer to the question you have heard.

Example:

You will hear: (Man) How do you go to school every day?
(Woman) Usually by bus. Sometimes by taxi.

TONE: How does the woman go to school?

You will read: A. She always goes to school on foot.
B. She usually takes a bike.
C. She takes either a bus or a taxi.
D. She usually goes to school by bus, never by taxi.

The best answer to the question "How does the woman go to school?" is C: "She takes either a bus or a taxi." Therefore, you should choose answer C.

Please go to the next page.

31. A. Six o'clock.
    B. Seven o'clock.
    C. Eight o'clock.
    D. Eight-thirty.

32. A. Driver.
    B. Construction worker.
    C. Mechanic.
    D. Plumber.

33. A. Vegetables.
    B. Cereal and vegetables.
    C. Cereals and bananas.
    D. Rice and mashed vegetables.

34. A. He publishes newspapers.
    B. He is an author.
    C. He collects automobiles.
    D. He works in industry.

35. A. He made money at first.
    B. He can't sell books.
    C. He and his boss get along well.
    D. He prefers to be a fireman.

36. A. Setting the table.
    B. Polishing silver.
    C. Sewing napkins.
    D. Stocking a pantry.

37. A. Her son was slapped.
    B. Her son is a troublemaker.
    C. Her son has bad grades.
    D. The teacher isn't competent.

38. A. In another building.
    B. In his office.
    C. In the bathroom.
    D. In a meeting.

39. A. 160 lbs.
    B. 150 lbs.
    C. 163 lbs.
    D. 153 lbs.

40. A. Mow the lawn.
    B. Weed the flowers.
    C. Pay $50 a month for a gardener.
    D. Work in the flower beds.

41. A. The man and woman shopped all over town.
    B. The woman went to many different stores.
    C. The woman bought some bookcases on sale.
    D. The man sold the woman some expensive bookcases.

42. A. He read the newspaper.
    B. One of his students told him.
    C. He listened to a radio report.
    D. He attended a cabinet meeting.

43. A. Herself.
    B. Mabel Anderson.
    C. The man.
    D. Marty.

44. A. His father is sick.
    B. He doesn't like school.
    C. He causes a lot of trouble.
    D. He's a poor student.

45. A. Lawyer.
    B. Detective.
    C. Policeman.
    D. Psychiatrist.

Part D

In Part D, you will hear 15 short talks. After each talk, you will hear a question about the talk. After you hear the question, read the four possible answers in your test book and choose the best answer to the question you have heard.

Example:

<u>You will hear:</u> Well, that's all for Unit 15. For today's homework, please do the review questions on page 80, and we'll check the answers tomorrow. Now, let's go on to Unit 16.

TONE: What is the teacher going to do next in today's class?

<u>You will read:</u>

A. Check the homework.
B. Review Unit 15.
C. Start a new unit.
D. Answer students' questions.

The best answer to the question "What is the teacher going to do next in today's class?" is C: "Start a new unit." Therefore, you should choose answer C.

Please go to the next page. ⇨

46. A. Men.
    B. Aboriginal men.
    C. Women.
    D. Aboriginal women.

47. A. A gun.
    B. A knife.
    C. A bomb.
    D. A club.

48. A. Tipping in restaurants.
    B. Different kinds of restaurants.
    C. A good restaurant.
    D. A self-service restaurant.

49. A. 27.
    B. 16.
    C. None.
    D. The speaker does not tell.

50. A. A driver and five passengers.
    B. A driver and five pedestrians.
    C. Five pedestrians.
    D. Two drivers.

51. A. American film making.
    B. American values.
    C. Early American life.
    D. Western films.

52. A. Italian music.
    B. Western music.
    C. Western opera.
    D. Romantic opera.

53. A. A home for old Victorians.
    B. A restaurant.
    C. A home for hundreds of paying guests.
    D. A home for a few paying guests.

54. A. Buying theater tickets well in advance.
    B. Buying theater tickets at the box office.
    C. Going to the theaters in Taipei.
    D. Last-minute discounts on theater tickets.

55. A. Bonn.
    B. Munich.
    C. Vienna.
    D. London.

56. A. A bus driver.
    B. A hotel clerk.
    C. A tour guide.
    D. A traveller.

57. A. A baseball player.
    B. Stephen Yang.
    C. A couch.
    D. A sportscaster.

58. A. Arriving passengers.
    B. Departing passengers.
    C. People boarding a boat.
    D. People departing from a train.

59. A. A child.
    B. A bear.
    C. An author.
    D. A pig.

60. A. Famous athletes.
    B. Televised sports.
    C. Sports news.
    D. Reporters.

中級英語聽力檢定測驗答案紙

中文姓名 ____________________　　　　測驗日期：民國 _____ 年 _____ 月 _____ 日

1. 准考證號碼					2. 出生 年(民國)		月		日		3. 國民身分證統一編號									
請依序將每個數字在下欄塗黑																				
0	0	0	0	0	0	0	0	0	0	0	A	0	0	0	0	0	0	0	0	0
1	1	1	1	1	1	1	1	1	1	1	B	1	1	1	1	1	1	1	1	1
2	2	2	2	2	2	2		2	2	2	C	2	2	2	2	2	2	2	2	2
3	3	3	3	3	3	3		3	3	3	D	3	3	3	3	3	3	3	3	3
4	4	4	4	4	4	4		4		4	E	4	4	4	4	4	4	4	4	4
5	5	5	5	5	5	5		5		5	F	5	5	5	5	5	5	5	5	5
6	6	6	6	6	6	6		6		6	G	6	6	6	6	6	6	6	6	6
7	7	7	7	7	7	7		7		7	H	7	7	7	7	7	7	7	7	7
8	8	8	8	8	8	8		8		8	I	8	8	8	8	8	8	8	8	8
9	9	9	9	9	9	9		9		9	J	9	9	9	9	9	9	9	9	9

K L M N O P Q R S T U V W X Y Z

＊注意：本答案紙限用 #2 (HB) 黑色鉛筆在「○」內塗黑、塗滿。

作答樣例：正確　　錯誤

正確：A B ● D

錯誤：A B ✓ D／A B ✕ D／A B ○ D／A B ◕ D

聽力測驗				
試題別				
試題冊號碼				

1 A B C D	11 A B C D	21 A B C D	31 A B C D	41 A B C D	51 A B C D
2 A B C D	12 A B C D	22 A B C D	32 A B C D	42 A B C D	52 A B C D
3 A B C D	13 A B C D	23 A B C D	33 A B C D	43 A B C D	53 A B C D
4 A B C D	14 A B C D	24 A B C D	34 A B C D	44 A B C D	54 A B C D
5 A B C D	15 A B C D	25 A B C D	35 A B C D	45 A B C D	55 A B C D
6 A B C D	16 A B C D	26 A B C D	36 A B C D	46 A B C D	56 A B C D
7 A B C D	17 A B C D	27 A B C D	37 A B C D	47 A B C D	57 A B C D
8 A B C D	18 A B C D	28 A B C D	38 A B C D	48 A B C D	58 A B C D
9 A B C D	19 A B C D	29 A B C D	39 A B C D	49 A B C D	59 A B C D
10 A B C D	20 A B C D	30 A B C D	40 A B C D	50 A B C D	60 A B C D

心得筆記欄

||||||||||||||||● 學習出版公司門市部 ●||||||||||||||||

台北地區：台北市許昌街 10 號 2 樓 TEL:(02)2331-4060·2331-9209
台中地區：台中市綠川東街 32 號 8 樓 23 室
TEL:(04)2223-2838

|||||||||||||||||||||||||||||||||||||||||||||||||||||||||

中級英語聽力檢定①（教學專用本）

主　　編／劉　毅
發 行 所／學習出版有限公司　☎ (02) 2704-5525
郵撥帳號／0512727-2 學習出版社帳戶
登 記 證／局版台業 *2179* 號
印 刷 所／裕強彩色印刷有限公司
台北門市／台北市許昌街 10 號 2 F　☎ (02) 2331-4060·2331-9209
台中門市／台中市綠川東街 32 號 8 F 23 室　☎ (04) 2223-2838
台灣總經銷／紅螞蟻圖書有限公司　☎ (02) 2795-3656
美國總經銷／Evergreen Book Store　☎ (818) 2813622
本公司網址　www.learnbook.com.tw
電子郵件　learnbook@learnbook.com.tw

售價：新台幣一百二十元正

2003 年 11 月 1 日一版五刷

ISBN 957-519-524-8

版權所有・翻印必究